Thorn of Bexar

Robert Wuench & Howard Carman

Reelfoot Publishing, Solon, OH

Authors' Notes:

This is a work of fiction. Though many of the characters and historical events described in this book are real, some even legendary or infamous, others are simply imagined. We have created relationships, supplied dialogue, modified time lines and invented certain details to tell a story we think could have happened. We hope this tale will inspire readers to learn more about what actually took place between 1800 and 1875 in the United States.

Italicized text "in quotation" represents insofar as possible the actual historic comments or writings of those to whom it is attributed.

ISBN: 978-0615642857

Published by *Reelfoot Publishing*, Solon, OH: ReelfootPublishing@gmail.com

Design and layout by *Born Too Late Design*: BornTooLateDesign@gmail.com

Printed in the United States of America

Authors' Acknowledgements:

We are grateful, first of all, to our wives who encouraged us to keep working on the project. They wanted us to finish at least *something* we'd started.

And our most sincere thanks go to our editors, Nancy Montwieler, Andrea Patters, and Mary Nease who took our raw material and suggested numerous enhancements to the manuscript to make sure we presented a correct, concise and readable story.

Several persons read the edited manuscript prior to publication. Dr. Lydia Mays of Georgia State University, Dr. Joachim Mayer of Case Western Reserve University and Bill Franks, Vice President of the Houston Preservation Society. All provided valuable critiques, convincing us that we had written "Thorn of Béxar" as close to historical truth as we had intended.

Judy Darrow gave us input for visualization, and several of our readers, as Judy did, told us we needed maps. The graphics and layout talent of Michael Wuench, "Born Too Late Design," created the cover, maps and provided the portrait of Emily West as we envisioned her, as well as the overall book layout.

Captain Nick Perugini, NOAA (Ret.) gave us insight into maritime hazards, ship capabilities in the 1800s and Atlantic sailing routes of the period. And the Hanings, Dale and Rosie, made sure we saw Indian Key to properly detail the voyage of the *Flash* in and around the Florida Keys.

Lastly we could not have told this story without the valuable resources and material available publicly from the University of Texas Library, [Texas] State Preservation Society, US Naval Archives, Wikipedia, 37th (Texas) Cavalry website, City of San Antonio records and countless others.

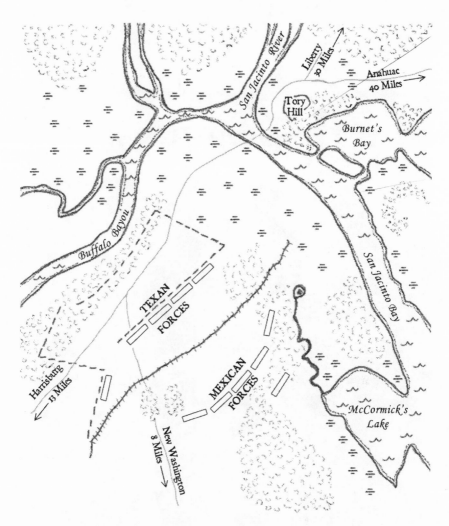

The Battle of San Jacinto: 21st April, 1836

Thorn of Béxar

Emily Morgan - Emily D. West

Prologue

"We hold these truths to be self-evident - that all men are created equal - that they are endowed by their Creator with certain inalienable rights - that among these rights are Life, Liberty and the Pursuit of Happiness."

(US Declaration of Independence - 4th July 1776)

~

4th July 1826: it had been fifty years since the Declaration of Independence from England, and in Philadelphia, the spirit of liberty was thriving. Celebrants crowded every open space - plazas, walkways and streets. Fireworks crackled, startling the horses drawing open carriages along the cobblestone pavement. In the distance a military band could be heard rehearsing for the evening festivities at the State House where the first Continental Congress had met and where fifty years earlier the Declaration of Independence had been signed. The State House Bell, its small cracks drilled out to prevent further expansion, was set to ring once again from the tower. The *USS Constitution,* *"Old Ironsides,"* affectionately nicknamed by her crew when they saw British eighteen-pound cannonballs bounce off her hull in the War of 1812, lay at anchor in the Delaware River. Most of her crew celebrated ashore, but the gunners of the President's Battery remained on board, ready to render the ship's salute to the nation.

This was, though, a celebration too quickly tempered with sadness as news traveled throughout the city that former President John Adams had died that morning. Flags fluttered at half-staff in the hot July breeze, providing room above each for the invisible flag of death. It took several days more for the news to reach Philadelphia that former President Thomas Jefferson too had died on 4th July 1826 at Monticello, his Virginia estate - a historic irony that these two men who, more than all others were responsible for the Declaration of Independence, would die 50 years to the day after the enactment of that document.

Four decades later the growing country would again be torn by war:

"...a great civil war, testing whether that nation, or any nation, so conceived and so dedicated can long endure."

(President Abraham Lincoln - Gettysburg Address)

Between the Revolutionary War and the Civil War came other seminal conflicts in 19th century American history - the War of 1812, the 1836 war for Texas Independence and the Mexican-American War of 1846. These events were pivotal to finally throwing off the English colonial yoke in the east and expanding the new nation in the west.

Legends grew around men and events of the period. Andrew Jackson, David Crockett and Sam Houston famously left their marks on history. General Lopez de Santa Anna, charismatic, self-proclaimed Emperor of Mexico, became the villain. Jean Lafitte and his protégé, Renato Beluche, were infamous pirates, but they fought for the US in the Battle of New Orleans. Neither the heroes nor the villains were as illustrious, or as incendiary, as their legends would have us believe.

"Thorn of Béxar" is about men of power, some who shaped a new nation, some who fought to keep their historic empire, some who fought for human dignity...and some who just liked a good fight - a story about people of many nationalities, races and persuasions in convergence and conflict - and about one woman who wielded more historical influence than she ever knew.

Emily Morgan West has existed in relative obscurity until now, perhaps because, as a female of mixed-race, historians largely ignored her. Yet she almost singlehandedly changed the course of Texas history, and her striking appearance inspired one of America's enduring folk songs. Emily West stopped Santa Anna's army at San Jacinto, and she was *"The Yellow Rose of Texas."*

"Remember the Alamo...remember Goliad!"

(Texas Army of the Republic and Volunteer militias - Battle of San Jacinto – 1836)

Chapter One

November 1811

"We have met the enemy and they are ours."

(US Navy Lieutenant Charles Oliver Hazard Perry – Battle of Lake Erie –War of 1812)

New Haven, Connecticut: her mother labored heavily through the afternoon to finally push the baby through the birth canal - excruciating pain, cold sweat, anguished moaning - *this birth didn't feel like the others. Something was terribly wrong!* The midwife struggled with her duties, finally grasping and twisting the baby by the head and shoulders, to deliver a beautiful, noisy mixed-race infant. *But there was too much blood around, and the mother was no longer moving.*

Early the next morning, Phineas Miller, father of the baby girl, received the news of her birth - and the death of her mother, *and he grieved silently for both.* Anna had been a freeperson in the employ of Miller and his business partner, Eli Whitney. The business was prospering, thanks to cotton gins and weapons parts for the army and local militias. But he could not afford the public scandal of an illegitimate child. *Was the child even his? How could Miller tell his wife? Where now could this child live? What kind of life did she face - her mother gone and her presumed father too prominent in New Haven, as well as Georgia, to accept responsibility for a mulatto child?* Fifteen years earlier in Georgia, Phineas Miller, a plantation superintendent, had married his employer, Catherine Littlefield Greene, the widow of Revolutionary War general, Nathaniel Greene.

Three months later, an unadorned, curtained carriage entered the sprawling Virginia estate, Monticello, and continued along the pathway until it drew up near the main servant's quarters, close by the Jefferson residence. Thomas Jefferson was about to have an unplanned addition to his slave population. And Baby Emily, as she had been named by the mid-wife, was making her first reluctant move toward influencing history. Phineas Miller, desperate to put matters right for the child, had imposed on his wife's close relationship with the former president to give the illegitimate child a proper home. Miller was discreetly assured, via a note from Thomas Jefferson's own quill pen, that Sally Hemings, with whom the former president enjoyed a similar illicit relationship, would treat Emily as one of their own.

The new slave child in the care of the Jefferson household was less than four months old when twelve British warships took up battle stations in Lake Ontario, giving England a strategic advantage as the War of 1812 began. Proper military strategy would then have dictated that the Americans blockade the Saint Lawrence Seaway, making it impossible for the formidable naval power of the British Empire to resupply itself. But the US initially would choose to fight the battle on Lake Erie and in western Ontario because war with England was more popular in that region. The English had been supplying local Indian tribes with guns and knives, hindering US northwestern expansion.

As Baby Emily was taking her first wobbly steps around the kitchens of Monticello on feet that would someday carry her to change the course of history, a 4,000 man American amphibious force sailed from Fort Niagara, New York under cover of darkness and fog and quietly anchored just west of the mouth of the Niagara River on the Canadian side. Marine infantry stormed Fort George, Ontario in a surprise attack, seizing the huge wood-stockade structure quickly as Lieutenant Oliver Hazard Perry, all the while, bombarded the wooden bulwark from his flotilla of sixteen schooners in the Niagara River. On his orders the gunners heated cannonballs until red hot, then quickly fired on the wooden fortress, creating an intense firestorm. When the Americans were finally driven off the peninsula late that year, they used fire again, this time to torch the entire nearby village of Newark, leaving Canadian civilians living there to die at the hands of a harsh winter.

This second war with England would eventually be fought on three fronts - around the Great Lakes, in the northeast around Baltimore and Washington and in the south, mainly around New Orleans. There would be battles on the high seas, giving rise to great warships - the *USS Constitution* carrying fifty-five cannons, including her main battery of six massive twenty-four pounders, and *HMS Africa* carrying sixty-four eighteen pounders. And land battles were fought in Baltimore at Fort McHenry and New Orleans where General Andrew Jackson earned his fame. The British Army in 1814 sacked the US Capitol in Washington and burned the White House, as well as the Capitol building. The US would prevail over England again, but not without mercenaries and local militias with people of all colors and heritages…sometimes questionable…coming to aid the fight. By the time it was over, little Emily was walking and talking in both English and Spanish, and the first of four wars waged in her lifetime would be history. Who would have suspected what an impact she would have in the coming battles?

From the beginning Sally Hemings knew that *this newcomer was no ordinary child.* As early as age six young Emily Miller already had a facility with words and language - she had mastered rudimentary Spanish at about the same time she was learning her first words in English - *who was she babbling with - the Dominican gardeners* - wondered Hemings. And the child loved books. She began reading almost as soon as she could talk, and the subject matter was of little consequence. Emily was interested in everything - and she forgot nothing that she heard, saw or read.

As she grew, the girl pestered Sally Hemings until the woman agreed to tutor her in French, a language she had learned herself while in the company of Jefferson as Ambassador to France. Helping prepare food and baking quickly became favorite household tasks of the young, increasingly beautiful 12-year old. Hemings taught Emily Miller as much as she could, concentrating on one of her own specialties - European style tortes and petit fours.

But the young girl could also be a problem. Something in her makeup caused Emily Miller to be aggressive - stubborn - even manipulative, traits that would, though, prove beneficial to her influence on later events. Barely into her 13th year she was already strikingly attractive and arrogantly aloof. *Yes this girl was sensual, industrious and intelligent. And she had a mind of her own. God only knew where she got that attitude!*

Emily Miller knew where she was headed in life - even if no one else did.

Chapter Two

July 1826

In Philadelphia, a lacquered black carriage, its brass fittings and sides reflecting the intense afternoon sun, drew to a halt on the pebbled drive in front of the Morgan Mansion. There was only a slight breeze, and not a drop of rain had fallen since late May. The lone occupant unlatched the carriage door and stepped quickly down without waiting for the liveried driver to attend him properly. Captain James Morgan, cutaway coattails flying behind him, took the steps to the veranda of his home two at a time - *relieved to be back from his hot and dusty trip to Virginia for the President's funeral.*

Once inside the foyer, handing over his tricorne and gloves to his valet, Morgan lost no time calling a young mixed-race woman into his study to recount the details of his travels - his viewing of the former President's body as it lay in state - then his attendance at the church service, graveside ritual and burial of Thomas Jefferson. Emily Morgan grieved as she listened intently - but with Jefferson now finally gone to rest, the young woman, not quite sixteen, knew that *her guardian of many years, Sally Hemings, would be legally free to leave Monticello and live the rest of her days with Eston, her son, in Charlottesville.* Emily Morgan had wanted to attend the funeral, pleaded with Captain Morgan to do so, but he'd countered, "Absolutely not - too much fodder for idle gossip."

Thomas Jefferson had granted three of Sally Hemings' children their freedom as soon as he himself had retired from the public eye and settled in his beloved Monticello. Later when Emily Miller was barely fifteen Jefferson had given the young girl her freedom, insistent that she leave Monticello and move to Philadelphia as a "freeperson," in the service of Captain James Morgan, a wealthy businessman. The captain had enthusiastically welcomed Emily into his household with virtually full family membership. Taking his family name, as was the custom, young Emily (Miller) Morgan was poised, beautiful and intelligent - olive-skinned and petite, yet sinuous and lean from her upbringing in the country at Monticello. Her dark hair, shining against steel blue eyes, made her a visual rarity. Emily (Miller) Morgan stood out in any gathering. "A little naïve but tough as rawhide," Captain Morgan would say to frequent influential callers who might find themselves enthralled with Morgan. "She can handle a blade like a butcher and she's not bad with a pistol either. So be really careful around her, boys. She won't take kindly to your usual monkey business."

Already a noted patriot and veteran of the 1812 war with England, tall, pale and soft-spoken James Morgan was a close friend to American and foreign diplomats and had influence with a wide range of politicians, businessmen and opportunists who swarmed through the growing northeast - including the recently-deceased former president and framer of the US Constitution and Declaration of independence, Thomas Jefferson.

Captain Morgan like most men of his time had encountered his share of tragedies and personal loss along his way to success. He was a decorated survivor of the 1814 Battle of Baltimore, with more than a few lingering pains and scars to prove it. And Morgan's wife had died two years earlier - a victim of her own battle with a swiftly fatal fever.

But as far as he knew himself, *Morgan had only two questionable habits. He liked fine Cuban cigars - just to chew - not to smoke. And he certainly liked a good shot of Irish whiskey or Jamaican rum straight up now and then - usually every day.*

Chapter Three

Fall 1830

It was raining and getting colder by the hour that late autumn afternoon when James Morgan received one of his many influential acquaintances, His Excellency Lorenzo de Zavala y Saenz, the former Mexican ambassador to Paris, in the library of his Philadelphia mansion.

De Zavala who was now living in exile in New York came from a far different background, but he and Morgan nevertheless shared common passions...*de Zavala, for Mexico to be free of its line of dictators and Spanish domination and Morgan for the new United States to rid the West of this same threat and form a nation that could eventually stretch from the Atlantic to the Pacific. Morgan and de Zavala were both aware of the vast lands and resources available in the Texas Territory to whoever could hold and populate them.*

As they sat sipping brandy from ornate crystal snifters after dinner, de Zavala spoke. "Señor Morgan, thank you for your kind hospitality on this damp and dismal evening and," raising his glass, "for this excellent brandy to stave off the chill. Let us get now to our business. I know your interests in seeing the Americas west of the Mississippi free themselves from Spanish and Mexican influence. You also know many people in the territories who feel passionate, as both you and I do about this matter. I have recently formed what we call the 'New Washington Association.' Perhaps you have heard of it - no?"

With a silent nod from Morgan who was as usual chewing an unlit cigar, de Zavala continued, emphasizing that this group of Western expansionists was strongly committed to freeing the Texas Territory once-and-for-all from Mexican influence. And their ultimate goal was to see it and other territories become part of a greatly expanded group of united states.

Morgan laid his cigar carefully in the ashtray at his side, pausing deliberately before he spoke. "Your Excellency, I have entertained similar thoughts to those you apparently harbor. Perhaps we can continue this important discussion soon and bring together a wider audience? For this evening I must say you have given me much to contemplate." In Morgan's mind *he needed to better understand de Zavala's true intent before putting any more of his own cards on the table.* De Zavala stood as the two men shook hands and de Zavala took his leave.

Some weeks later, on a crisp late October evening His Excellency Ambassador Lorenzo de Zavala e Saenz, dressed impeccably in a dark Regency cutaway jacket, white waistcoat and maroon velvet trousers - his honorary medals prominent on his lapels - was again James Morgan's dinner guest. The two men met with several other expansionist supporters who had been invited to James Morgan's estate. Dozens of candles in crystal chandeliers overhead lit the dark mahogany paneled dining room with a soft orange glow. A fire crackled in the cavernous stone fireplace at one end of the room. De Zavala, like his host James Morgan and the other men, had enjoyed a feast of roast venison, yams and local Indian corn followed by an elaborate dessert concoction and strong chicory coffee, all prepared by young Emily Morgan. Dabbing his chin contentedly, de Zavala now spoke effusively and eloquently about his loyalties to his adopted country and the direction he hoped to steer the future of the Tejas territory.

"I envision," said Ambassador de Zavala, "a time when Coahuila y Tejas is part of the great American West, and its immigrant people from all lands - Germany, Mexico, Ireland, England, Hispaniola and yes, Native American and Negro peoples as well, are all citizens of a new Republic of Texas.

"But to realize this dream we must first free Tejas from my former countrymen and their Spanish overlords who want to make all such land and wealth a part of Mexico forever. This is no small endeavor - we will need arms and men, supplies and transport. This will take money and time - time that I fear we have not so much of. There is little doubt that precious lives will be lost, but that is the price of freedom in this vast new land. The latest Mexican regime and their powerful army have grand designs in their heads for Tejas and perhaps all the Catholic territories of the West. I propose that we as the New Washington Association raise a military effort to help our Texian and Tejano friends defeat the Mexican army before matters get any worse!"

Lorenzo de Zavala's support for an independent Texas increased the odds of it happening ten fold, but could he be trusted? Was he a Mexican patriot - an American patriot - or simply amoral, a common traitor - an opportunist, Morgan thought to himself, as he listened to de Zavala's plea. He had reviewed the man's background in more detail since their last meeting. *De Zavala read, wrote and spoke fluent Spanish, English, and French. His mastery of Greek and Latin was on a level with the clergy. He was a statesman, soldier, already a Texas land impresario, a writer, an editor and a physician.*

Emily Morgan quietly eavesdropped on as much of the conversation as possible between Morgan, de Zavala and the other guests as she and the staff attended to the dinner guests. *Even though she had been around men of power and influence at Monticello, there was something different, something unique, about this exiled Mexican gentleman, de Zavala.*

Still listening, but with his mind more focused on the man than his latest comments, James Morgan, continued his musings. *De Zavala had developed an early interest in politics leading to a municipal government position in 1812. In 1813, he published his first newspaper. Arrested later during the purge of liberals after the restoration of Spain's Ferdinand VII, he used his three-year imprisonment to learn English and study medicine. He practiced medicine after his release from prison until 1820 when he was elected a deputy to the Spanish Cortes. News of Mexico's break with Spain led de Zavala to abandon the Spanish court and return to Mexico to serve in the Constituent Congress of 1822 and the Mexican Senate. He remained in the national legislature until 1827, when he was elected governor of the state of Mexico. Subsequent*

*disillusionment with his mother country though, had resulted in his
now self-imposed US exile in New York.*

Morgan was amazed too that De Zavala was such a
prolific writer. *Where did he find the time?* He had helped
author Mexico's Constitution of 1824 and was now in the final
stages of a two-volume *"Ensayo historico de las revoluciones de
Mexico (Historical Essay on the Revolutions of Mexico)."* Earlier
this same year, de Zavala had completed another patriotic
work, lamenting the state of Mexico's fortunes. The predictive
prologue read:

> *"However, [this work] should be very useful to Mexicans, for
> it is to them that I dedicate it. In it they will find a true description
> of the people whom their legislators have tried to imitate - a people
> that is (sic) hard working, active, reflective, circumspect, religious in
> the midst of a multiplicity of sects - tolerant, thrifty, free, proud and
> persevering."*

~

Far to the south this same night, in the military
headquarters adjoining his presidential hacienda, Antonio de
Padua Maria Severino Lopez de Santa Anna y Perez de
LeBron, more familiarly, Generale Lopez de Santa Anna, sat at
one end of his war room table. Of only average height and
slight of build, Santa Anna made up for an unimposing
physique with perfectly tailored uniforms and an impressive
military bearing. His piercing, almost unblinking dark eyes
matched a thick shock of well-trimmed hair. Santa Anna was
clean-shaven, a hygienic preference from his years in the field
leading an army.

This particular evening he briefed the Mexican Army
general staff on their latest campaign to control the rebellious
peasants at home in Mexico and in "Mexico del Norte." *He had
no plans for Tejas to ever be part of the new America.* Santa Anna
had not risen to his position as Army Commander without
reason or influence. Several years before, then only a brash,

young colonel, his disciplined unit had routed Spanish forces from Vera Cruz.

Immediately after the battle Santa Anna had been promoted to Generale. With his promotion by the future emperor, Augustine de Iturbide, came the additional grant of a sizeable hacienda, "Manga de Clavo", near the city Santa Anna had saved. Eventually Spain capitulated in an attempt to conserve its far-flung resources defending its empire. And now, with Santa Anna self-installed as the Army leader, Spain and Mexico forged an uneasy alliance, protecting their North American territories west of the Mississippi from Anglo expansion.

Over a remarkably short time Emperor de Iturbide proved to be a complete disappointment. And Santa Anna, *never one to worry about which cause he supported so long as he was on the winning side*, conspired with Vicente Guerrero and Lorenzo de Zavala y Saenz, the Mexican Ambassador to France, to overthrow the government. Too soon though the revolving "coup d'etat" door spun again. Vicente Guerrero was deposed and summarily executed. A new puppet emperor, Anastasio Bustamante, appeared in the palace in Mexico City - put there largely by Lopez de Santa Anna and the power of the Mexican Army. Santa Anna was now in command of all Mexican forces, and some had now declared him "Napoleon de Mexico!" Santa Anna *disliked the comparison immensely, disgusted by what Napoleon had done to subjugate much of Spain*. Even so at this point Santa Anna *considered himself the de-facto ruler of Mexico and Coahuila de Tejas Territory*. Mexico had become a full-fledged, powerful military dictatorship, threatening to permanently block the colonization and consolidation of the west by eastern US expansionists.

De Zavala had quickly fallen out of favor with Lopez de Santa Anna and his new emperor, Anastasio Bustamente. *De Zavala was far too concerned about the welfare of the general population* for Santa Anna's liking, *and Emperor Bustamante had to agree*. From de Zavala's perspective *there was simply no stability, no structure for the future that Mexico and its unfortunate citizens could build on.* All they could hope for, in Zavala's mind, was a serf-like existence while the country's leaders continued to drain the coffers with attendant wars, rebellions, coups and corruption. Mexico was indeed enduring its *"Era of Coups,"* but to quote Santa Anna, *"A hundred years to come my people will not be fit for liberty. They do not know what it is, unenlightened as they are, and under the influence of a Catholic clergy. A despotism is the proper government for them, but there is no reason why it should not be a wise and virtuous one."*

Now fearing for his life, de Zavala sought sanctuary in the French ambassador's residence during a state dinner honoring the latest Mexican puppet emperor and his powerful army commander. At the French ambassador's insistence, *recognizing Excellency de Zavala's dedication to the cause of eternal friendship between Mexico and France,* Emperor Bustamante reluctantly granted de Zavala safe passage out of Mexico - despite the vocal objections of Generale Lopez de Santa Anna. De Zavala then made his way by sea to Baltimore, after briefly disembarking in the recently settled port of New Washington, Texas - situated strategically on a bluff overlooking San Jacinto Bay. It was there in a small back room of the town hall that de Zavala conferred with independence-minded Tejanos and Texians. And it was during this brief stopover that de Zavala had formed the idea for the New Washington Association.

Mexico was indeed in a state of rebellion and political instability that could be exploited by strong army leadership, and Generale Santa Anna repeatedly stepped into - indeed enlarged the chaos, using it to his advantage. With such instability, Mexico and its powerful, seasoned land army represented a considerable strategic threat to those in the fledgling "united states" who would expand their own empire westward. Zavala pondered all this with consternation as he sat in the ship tender being rowed out to a schooner at New Washington. *He needed to ready himself for a life outside his native country somewhere in the east - in the new America. His former countrymen and Tejano patriots needed a new direction, strong leadership and strategic support if Mexico and the new America were to long survive, side-by-side.*

Chapter Four

October 1833

"There are two things a democratic people will always find very difficult – to begin a war and to end it."

(Alexis de Tocqueville)

The two young Frenchmen, Alexis de Tocqueville, 25, and Gustave de Beaumont, 28, had arrived in the United States two years earlier to study the American prison system. Both were also intrigued with the notion of American democracy and eager to see as much as they dared of the new country. Their early travels took them through New York State and Michigan, as well as parts of Canada, before they returned to the east coast in early October of 1833.

They were treated like royalty everywhere as they met with prominent and influential leaders of the day. Meeting with Charles Carroll, the last surviving signer of the Declaration of Independence, de Tocqueville expressed the admiration of his countrymen for the American constitutional process. Carroll, one of the wealthiest men in Maryland, was the only one of the 56 signers of the Declaration of Independence who was Roman Catholic, de Tocqueville's professed religion. With de Beaumont, de Tocqueville then made his way to Philadelphia, and by mid-October, arrived for a two-week stay. De Tocqueville planned to visit Eastern State Penitentiary in nearby Cherry Hills.

Through his many local contacts in Philadelphia, James Morgan had learned of the de Tocqueville visit *and was determined to make the man's acquaintance.* Morgan's interest lay *in seriously enlisting the young Frenchman's influential support in his native country for the New Washington Association. French help* Morgan determined *might be beneficial in freeing Texas from Mexican and Spanish dominance.*

It was a tribute to James Morgan's international reputation and the presence of the former Mexican Ambassador to France, Lorenzo de Zavala y Saenz, when the two men accepted Morgan's invitation to the equivalent of a State dinner at his mansion. This time several wives and female companions were also in attendance. On the appointed date de Tocqueville and de Beaumont were driven to the property. It was another cold, misty fall evening. Shivering outside the door to the mansion, de Tocqueville and de Beaumont were soon overwhelmed, and their Frenchmens' hearts warmed considerably, when a beautiful young mixed-race woman, dressed in the latest Continental evening wear, welcomed them to the Morgan residence in reasonably fluent French - *by Parisian standards,* they thought.

"Les gentilshommes, soyez bienvenus aux États-Unis, à Philadelphie et à l'état Morgan. Je suis Emily Morgan, un membre de la maison de Capitaine James Morgan. Or, if you prefer English, may I say, gentlemen, welcome to the United States, to Philadelphia, and to the Morgan estate. I am Emily Morgan, a member of the household of Captain James Morgan. It is our privilege to have such distinguished men of our ally, France, in our presence. Captain Morgan asks that you please advise if there is anything that you wish me to undertake to make your visit more enjoyable." As Emily Morgan spoke the welcome, she made a slight, deferential bow to de Tocqueville and de Beaumont.

"Mademoiselle, the pleasure we assure you is ours," responded de Tocqueville as he doffed his top hat, bowed and his pursed lips properly grazed her outstretched right hand. "And please do not tempt me. Where may I ask did you acquire such elegant command of our mother tongue?"

"My parents lived in Paris for a period of time some years ago, and I learned, at my own insistence, many of the nuances of your elegant tongue upon their return to the United States," Morgan effortlessly fibbed.

"They and you are to be commended. We have visited New York, Boston, most of Michigan, and eastern Canada, and our itinerary includes further travel to Baltimore, Cincinnati, New Orleans and Washington. However you make M. de Beaumont and me feel that Philadelphia should have already become our new residence outside of France."

~

With the guests now all arrived and lodged in their respective rooms and dressing for dinner, Emily Morgan herself changed into her chef's attire and turned to her usual tasks - banquet preparation in the cavernous kitchen of the Morgan mansion and the direction of the 5-person kitchen staff. Together they had to prepare, serve and later dispose of the remnants of yet another varied and extravagant evening meal.

Morgan pondered deeply as she worked. *I heard Master Morgan and his Excellency Ambassador de Zavala, along with M. de Tocqueville, discussing President Jefferson and President Adams' deaths, and all that has happened since then. Even though we have much to be thankful for here as freepersons in Philadelphia, there is much to be done in the western territories they speak of. Ambassador de Zavala says Mexico wants to keep much of the land west of the Mississippi River that rightfully should be part of our country. There are many people in Tejas who want to be part of our country rather than Mexico, and too, there is much land and gold that Mexico and Spain should not lay claim to. I think he makes a lot of sense. He seems a very persuasive man - quite dashing and handsome! To me he is the typical Latin male - darkly romantic and mysterious.* And Morgan let one added thought find its way into her consciousness - *but I wonder why he is attracted to the blond woman, Madame West, who is with him and he has introduced as his fiancé? She seems to me nothing more than a spoiled New York society girl.*

One of the staff, Eliza, born a freeperson in Philadelphia and sheltered in the Morgan household since birth, interrupted Morgan's private thoughts with several *mundane* questions about the sequence of dinner servings and which of the guests needed special attention. Emily Morgan responded fully to the kitchen maid's queries, but Eliza could tell that *Miss Emily was preoccupied with somethin' really serious.* Eliza, like the rest of the kitchen staff, would have been even more surprised had they known Emily Morgan's further unspoken thoughts.

I am not of this household - never will be! My heritage is that of presidents, and Monticello is my home.

No one ever told me where I came from. Mama Hemings was not my real mother – of that I am certain. But she is the closest relation I've got. And I am still somehow angry that Captain Morgan would not let me attend Thomas Jefferson's funeral. Even though we've never spoken of it, he must know my entire story and what President Jefferson meant to me. After all, it was he and Mama Hemings who recognized that it was time for me, for my own protection, to leave Monticello. Thomas Jefferson himself made the arrangements for me to move to Philadelphia to work for Captain Morgan.

My God will I ever be able to put behind me why I had to leave? One of his influential plantation owner friends who lived a day's ride away was finally an overnight guest at Monticello. I recall this man, John Smith, only as a complete bastard! He was short and of a rather heavy build, like a bulldog - several chins. His long mutton chops and mustache seemed to have not been recently trimmed or cleaned, and his hair was thinning noticeably. He dressed finely, but nothing, not even his boots fit properly. He did have nice teeth, but they seemed out of place in a small, thin-lipped mouth that always had a snarl at the edge. What the President saw in him - other than money - I never knew.

Mr. Smith I believe had decided the first time he saw me that he wanted to have me for his own sexual pleasures. After dinner

President Jefferson had him meet with Mama Hemings and me to discuss his chamber needs. One requirement was he insisted I serve him his morning coffee, bacon and biscuits in his room. Mama Hemings had to agree, but warned me to be very careful of Mr. Smith

The next morning I took his tray in with his breakfast and turned to leave. He grabbed me and one hand went quickly between my legs. He was strong - he threw me onto the bed and was on top of me, ripping my skirt away and exposing his erect member. I yelled - I screamed, and fortunately Mama Hemings came running with a kitchen cleaver. In Smith's embarrassment and fear, his member shriveled and he quickly dismounted me and began to pull up his trousers. All the while I heard Mama Hemings shouting that if he touched me again, she would kill him.

That whole incident, I was told, was quite embarrassing to the President, but he did nothing to alienate this bastard, John Smith. He had too much money and power to be sent away. So instead President Jefferson and Mama Hemings decided it was time for me to go to work for Captain James Morgan here in Philadelphia. I would have a better life because the city has a large freeperson population, and the Quakers, who helped found the city, do not support slavery. When I think now about it, maybe I was becoming a problem for President Jefferson? Maybe Mama Hemings knew that it was best that I leave? In any case, I am now free. I have left the South and I have a new future.

So had it begun - Emily Miller, born in New Haven, a motherless child, then Emily Morgan via President Jefferson in Monticello, was now in Philadelphia serving dinner to people who she would later stand with as an equal on the field of battle. She tasted this latest move from the confines and intrigue of Monticello to the excitement and uncertainty of life in Philadelphia *like fresh cold strawberries on a summer morning. There were great events brewing in the new United States, and talk was everywhere of expansion west. She was ready to be part of whatever lay ahead.* And she was to be a major pawn in the game.

~

News traveled over the next several months from Philadelphia, New York and Washington through the former colonies and territories that James Morgan and Lorenzo de Zavala were recruiting men and gathering materiel for the fight brewing with Mexico for territories west of the Mississippi. At home in Virginia John Smith was not beyond helping this effort - in fact he welcomed the opportunity. Smith was a man of money and means. He knew others who could help, too. He had been Jefferson's friend, though they'd had their disagreements over certain issues - most of them having to do with slavery. Yet he felt that *essentially he, Jefferson and Morgan were cut from the same unwavering patriotic cloth.*

And another matter - hadn't Jefferson dispatched that pretty little slave, Emily, to the Morgan household, presumably to get her away from him? He was never going to forget that incident! There had to be a way to even the score against her and that equally insolent Hemings woman! Just who the hell did they think they were? They were property, to be used at the pleasure of their owners. If even Presidents exercised such rights, why shouldn't he?

By God it was time for action! He'd simply contact Morgan and de Zavala, offer his services and in the end require that Emily Morgan be part of his compensation from the organizers. Then she would be part of the Smith household, and be beholden to no one but him. She was truly the prettiest, most desirable young mulatto he'd ever seen. She'd be a perfect bed companion for a few years…until her ass spread and she got jowly, like the Negro women always did. In any event for now he needed to have a respite from some of his more questionable business associates and personal relationships in Virginia. No one had threatened him - not yet anyway, but he knew people who had disappeared in the new country for transgressions less questionable than some of his.

North in Philadelphia some weeks later, Emily Morgan discreetly overheard the latest dinner talk around the Morgan dinner table, as Captain Morgan briefed yet another meeting of the New Washington Association on the progress of assembling and funding an expedition westward to Tejas. The de Tocqueville party was not present, although the Frenchmen had left a sizeable influence on the gathering and already pledged their support to the venture.

Morgan was speaking, "We have a seaworthy schooner, the '*Flash*' and a seasoned crew. It will take us south around the Florida Keys and into the Gulf. We can stop in both the Florida and Louisiana territories for provisions before heading on to what we now call New Washington on the San Jacinto River...near the Tejas - let us say - 'Texas,' coast? His Excellency, Señor de Zavala is well familiar with New Washington and the Texas territories and can tell you more at our leisure after dinner.

"There are ample sources of personal firearms, cannon, and ammunition, as well as cutlasses. We have explosives, fresh and dried food sources and building materials that have been promised, as John Smith can elaborate. We will need hundreds of men and many women, and at least some who can speak Spanish if we are to be able to function, once we are in the western territory. Some of us are already working on that issue. I've heard certain reports too that there are many in the southern territories who are eager to volunteer their hunting and fighting skills in our effort. It will only take promises of cheap, arable land in Texas to get them to commit to our cause.

"And lastly thanks to you in this room and many others of like mind who have met with us earlier, we have the funds to support our expedition. Now may I present our newest Association member, Mr. John Smith of Virginia - friend of presidents, supporter of liberty, and with his vast network of business contacts, a worthy procurer of almost any provisions that could be needed."

Smith nodded without speaking. However, Emily Morgan, standing near the kitchen entrance, barely maintained her composure. She had already been *chagrined - disturbed, frustrated* - when Captain Morgan had informed her that John Smith would be with them as his houseguest for several days and was eventually joining the expedition to the west. *How could this pig have wormed his way into the Morgan household and thrust himself into what appeared to be a just cause for free people? And how long would it be before Smith knew she was part of Morgan's family and made similar demands of her to those he had made at Monticello? Frankly, he probably knew about her already. She had to find a way to control the situation - to protect herself.* As some of the oppression and hopelessness she'd once felt at Monticello crept back into her consciousness, a plan formed in Morgan's mind. *Its practicality pushed her dread aside.*

~

Morgan had spent much of the afternoon in the kitchen, overseeing the staff as they prepared yet another elegant dinner for Captain Morgan's New Washington Association members.

She pondered as she kneaded dough, *there must indeed be a great deal to talk about and plan if he and Ambassador de Zavala are to be successful in the West. And after dinner these men will probably drink and talk their way through yet another long night, before retiring in their exhausted and usually intoxicated stupors.*

When the time is right I intend to demonstrate my worth to this expedition. My knowledge of Spanish and French - my skills at provisioning, cooking and domestic organization and, yes, my ability with pistols and knives as defense weapons - don't they all make me a valuable expedition member? Certainly my looks, charm and manners have impressed Minister de Zavala, too? Now all that remains for this evening is to deal with Mr. Smith.

The thought of being with de Zavala for an extended journey and on such a great adventure lifted the young woman's spirits considerably as she prepared the desserts - pot au chocolat for most of the guests - *and to deal with her most immediate threat, her special Pontefract cakes for Mr. John (the bastard) Smith.*

Pontefract Cakes:
Boil licorice root for a few minutes and blanch it in cold water. Then drain it and chop into small cubes. Mix with crushed anise seed, finely chopped mint and laurel. Mash into a pulp or sauce. Season with cane sugar and salt. Blend this mixture into any fine biscuit dough and bake into small cakes
Coat them with some powdered cane sugar and butter melted together with Irish Whisky

As she stood in the ornate, heavily carved dining room doorway, Morgan graciously accepted the group's compliments for her dinner creations and the hard work of the mansion's kitchen staff, "An excellent meal, set off once again by the best desserts served in the East," remarked James Morgan - proud of his young, beautiful chef de cuisine from Paris, by way of Virginia. John Smith, though quiet enough, felt especially gratified *if not yet quite satisfied, to see that this beautiful but arrogant mulatto, who had rebuked him in Monticello, had now been required to prepare an especially spicy and tasty dessert solely for him in honor of his joining the Association. Damn, was that a flirtatious glance he caught from her as she helped with the clearing of the table?*

The gathering lasted another two hours, with extended talk of conflict in the west and how the New Washington Association would prevail. Cigars and pipes were brought out - James Morgan, as usual chewing an unlit Cubano while others smoked. Brandy and good Irish whiskey topped off the evening for an increasingly noisy gathering around the massive stone fireplace. Along with the others, John Smith finally said his "good nights" and unsteadily made his way to his quarters in the south wing of the Morgan mansion. *For some reason he now considered sleep more important than bedding that mulatto girl tonight? Why* he wondered silently. *Why?*

Pushing at his door handle Smith unexpectedly found Emily Morgan's petite bare foot and leg blocking his way as she slipped almost silently into the room beside him. Her ankle-length, full-pleated skirt was hiked up, revealing most of her smooth, olive-toned thigh. "Now Mr. Smith, I thought you gentlemen would never finish those long-winded discussions - all that talk of taking Tejas, or Texas or whatever it is, away from Mexico. I had better things for you to attend to tonight." John Smith was...quite simply...awestruck! *Here was the slave girl he'd lusted after, been scorned by, now in his room and looking so completely like she finally wanted him to take her. But even stranger - as much as his lust for her these past few months had consumed him, he felt little of it now. In fact there was a total absence of ardor as she pushed him aggressively toward the bed, then onto it and sat down beside him - one bare leg draped across his lap.*

Almost painfully Smith endured Morgan's breath in his ear and her whispered taunts as her bare left arm caressed his *fleshy, damp* shoulders. With the other hand she gently grasped the inside of his *meaty* thigh. Now she felt for and found his *disgusting* groin and its *limp* member. "Mr. Smith where IS my little friend! Has he forgotten his manners? I thought that now that you've found me, he'd want to be strong so he can play inside me?" Reflexively Smith's right arm flailed drunkenly, catching Morgan hard across the side of her face. Her ear and jaw stung, and the force of the blow sent her reeling into one corner of the room.

Now Smith was out of bed, confused, humiliated and beyond anger. Drawing his thick rawhide belt from his pant-loops, he tottered - *bowlegged* - toward the crumpled young woman just getting up off the floor - his belt in hand and drawn back to strike. Smith reasoned *it was high time, once and for all, that he taught this black bitch a lesson in subservience. Dammit all, maybe giving her a good whipping would even bring his old libido back!*

Smith heard the knife almost before he saw it - a soft, almost velvet-metallic *swush* as the biggest blade he'd ever seen appeared from somewhere within Emily Morgan's skirt folds, sliced through the air in her hand and drew blood from his forearm. "I thought you just wanted to PLAY John Smith - but if you want to play ROUGH, we can do that too." Morgan's voice was soft and even, but menacing - her eyes glinted - cold, greenish blue, matching the light reflecting off the blade she now held easily in one hand. *The few drops of blood at one corner of her mouth made her glare even more sinister. Captain Morgan already warned me about this girl and her knives, goddammit all! Now look at me...I'm cut! She'll likely butcher me like the hogs she used to gut for Jefferson, if I go at her more.*

"Get the hell out! We're through!" Smith groaned as he turned away and half-waved his free arm at her, motioning Morgan toward the door. Her barefoot exit was hardly noticed as an exhausted and humiliated Smith flopped onto his bed, holding his bloody arm. Wrapping bedclothes and his loose belt around the wound, Smith doused the bedside lamp and fell into a drunken and disturbed slumber, while Morgan in her room dabbed cold water at her bruised and swollen face and lip and smiled briefly to herself.

Chapter Five

Fall 1834

It was still dark on the Philadelphia docks where the schooner, *Flash,* was berthed. A rolling fog and cold mist made work outside in the pre-dawn of mid-October 1834 miserable for sailors and longshoremen alike. Astern in the main salon of the *Flash,* Captain Morgan conferred over maps with Lorenzo de Zavala, along with the ship's helmsman and Captain Robert Bonner, the commander of his hired vessel. They could hear the whining of block and tackles, the thumps of crates and pallets as groaning men struggled to load the hold. The cacophony of stevedores' manual labor was mixed with the normal creaks of the wood-hulled schooner, as harbor waves lapped against the side of the ship. On the *Flash* and the docks, preparations for the long voyage around Florida and on to Texas proceeded quickly.

The schooner had a galley, sleeping quarters and a head for its captain and a crew of five. All aboard shared the galley, but separate sleeping quarters and a head had been provided for James Morgan, Lorenzo de Zavala, and Emily Morgan - as well as her nemesis, John Smith. Several lesser members of the Morgan party would sleep in improvised discomfort, a cramped storage area behind the crew quarters.

With the ship captain's reluctant permission, Captain Morgan had quietly arranged for one 18-pound smooth bore cannon to be concealed in the bow, to be available in the event that warning fire might be needed to ward off a pirate attack. Though capable of carrying as many as 10 heavy cannons exposed on her decks, James Morgan suspected that *the Flash crew would not be willing to participate in firing upon or significant engagement with privateers or their raiding party. Jean Lafitte and his brother, Pierre, were long gone from these waters, but they had left their legacy up and down the east coast and in the gulf. If word got out that any in the crew of the Flash fired upon a ship out of the former Jean Lafitte fleet, they would most likely all be hunted down, drawn and quartered. Besides one or more crew could even be in league with coastal privateers.*

Enough water and food, including chickens and pigs, had been brought aboard to get the ship to Charleston, South Carolina. A barrel of rum would be shared by all. Morgan's stock of expensive, chewable Cuban cigars would not.

The *Flash* was two masted, with a wood hull, reinforced with steel. She was 80 feet long and 18 feet wide. Her loaded weight of 70 tons drafted only 10 feet, deep enough to be fairly stable in anything but high seas, but shallow enough that the *Flash* could travel reasonably close to the sand bars at Cape Hatteras and through the keys of south Florida. With a relatively light load, on a good day with a favorable current, and following wind under full sail, she could make 10 to 12 knots.

Captain Morgan and the crew of the *Flash* had the route arranged. The ship would sail from Philadelphia past Cape Hatteras, North Carolina - then call in Charleston, South Carolina, and if necessary, Jacksonville, Florida. After a longer call in Key West they'd cross the Gulf of Mexico to New Orleans, and finally Texas. The chosen route was a slower one, but would keep the ship closer to the shore in the event of bad weather. Also, fewer stores had to be loaded on board in Philadelphia in favor of taking on provisions further south from associates of John Smith.

Captain Bonner had considered sailing past Cape Hatteras directly toward Miami, bypassing Charleston, which charts showed was a shorter, much faster route. However using this route around Cape Hatteras, as the easternmost projection of land along the eastern seaboard, meant that a straight run to Miami could take the ship 100 miles or more off the coast of Georgia and Florida. The odds of a schooner the size of the *Flash* surviving a tropical storm or worse so far out to sea were not good.

The crew knew that first leg from Philadelphia to Cape Hatteras was likely to be the most dangerous part of the voyage. The warm Gulf Stream flowing north merged with the southerly-flowing North Atlantic current. This current forced southbound ships toward a dangerous twelve-mile sandbar where hundreds of shipwrecks had occurred in the well-named "Graveyard of the Atlantic." A 90-foot tall sandstone lighthouse, with a light powered by whale oil, had been constructed at Hatteras in 1803. Captain Bonner, commander of the *Flash*, knew its shortcomings well. *The lighthouse was unable to effectively warn ships of the dangerous sand bars and shoals because it was too short to be observed off-shore in normal transit, the unpainted sandstone blended in with the background, and the signal was not strong enough to reach mariners far out in open, rolling seas.*

The *Flash* eased out of Philadelphia harbor into the Delaware River, bound for the open Atlantic. Captain Bonner, a seasoned veteran of Atlantic and Gulf coastal waters was at the helm. Others stood on deck as the crew went about its duties and the outline of the city faded in the distance. Most were wondering *what lay ahead in the voyage around Florida and beyond.*

~

Three days out of Philadelphia brought the first rough seas to the *Flash* and her occupants. All but the crew were ordered to remain below deck where some were at ease in their sleeping hammocks, while one or two were too ill to think about anything but the *overwhelming nausea and fear of dying on the high seas.*

As she swung in her bunk, jaw and facial bruises almost faded now, Emily Morgan at last had resolved one of her concerns. As *soon as possible she would request Captain Morgan's permission to change her name. She did not want to be a Morgan, and she could not be a Miller. How had she gotten that name, anyway? Was someone named Miller her real father? It made no difference any more. There was no advantage to her old family name and, despite Captain Morgan's kindness, she did not want to be known as a Morgan - too many political and other influential connections to suit one who was seeking a new life. No she needed a new identity, and what better name to take than where she was heading now - West? That's it - Emily D West - the "D" a measure of her admiration of Excellency Lorenzo 'D' Zavala who sometimes used the same middle initial, occasionally dropping the more formal Hispanic "de" after he came to America.*

Manning the ship's wheel above, the helmsman had the considerable challenge of maintaining the *Flash's* heading in the gathering storm. All but one of the ship canvasses, a storm jib, had been doused and secured. The captain and three of the crew in heavy oils braved the rain and surging seas to man their stations. Lorenzo de Zavala and James Morgan, veterans of such sea encounters but not wishing to test their maritime skills, remained as directed in their quarters. John Smith however, fascinated by this new experience, donned his heaviest cloak, and despite objections from Captain Bonner, joined the three sailors manning the deck. He'd never seen or heard anything quite like the wind-whipped seas, lightning and thunder as a full-blown gale howled through the ship's rigging.

Standing at the starboard railing, having lashed himself loosely to a railing cleat with a line through his belt and about his ample waist as ordered, Smith felt secure but not calm. The storm, now near hurricane force, lashed at the schooner and quickly soaked Smith to the skin. Shivering uncontrollably, he pondered the roiling sea. *Its fury somehow reminded him vaguely of his recent confrontation with the slave girl. But wait, a new problem -* Smith noted with some anxiety *- briefly now, the deck itself seemed to lift in his direction, almost vertically* he thought, as the ship encountered a rogue wave. Never the steadiest afoot even when on solid ground, Smith felt his stocky legs buckling as both feet in his water-logged boots suddenly slipped from under him on the angled, drenched wooden planking. In an instant Smith found himself sliding, *silly…he* thought, against...*then OVER* the railing, and plunging headlong toward the looming foam. Smith's last earthly sensations were *the abrasive sting of his tether as it looped round his head then coiled itself tightly about his neck - and the pain...fading into...blinding light...as his now-jackknifed body whiplashed repeatedly against the schooner's hull.* Cries of "Man overboard!" were soon replaced by the hasty, chaotic act of retrieving Smith's body.

Smith's corpse lay face up on the rolling deck, as Captain Bonner and Lorenzo de Zavala examined the body for any signs of foul play. A concerned James Morgan looked on, chewing at a damp cigar. The captain had summoned de Zavala up from below decks, recognizing his practical background in medicine and earlier university physician's training in Ciudad de Mexico.

As the examination proceeded, the rain and wind seemed to abate. More passengers, including Emily Morgan, found their way into the now-chilling night air of the Atlantic to talk of Smith's untimely death. Though a healing knife-like wound on his right forearm was observed, there was no indication of any foul play that might have caused his demise. *Emily Morgan did not grieve.*

Noon the next day brought calmer waters and clearing skies with brisk westerly winds as a somber ceremony for John Smith began. As was the custom at sea, Captain Bonner first read from the Anglican Book of Common Prayer, *"I am the resurrection and the life, saith the Lord: he that believeth in me, though he were dead, yet shall he live: and whosoever believeth in me shall never die."* James Morgan added his remarks of respect for the first real casualty of the New Washington expedition. Then Smith's sailcloth-shrouded corpse, weighted at the feet with two cannon balls, slid down an uplifted mess table and disappeared into the waves. Like the others, Emily Morgan observed the ceremony *with appropriate outward reverence. He's gone and I am free of whatever proposition or demand he made to Captain Morgan - a waste of good ammunition, those two eighteen pounders - but good riddance. God help me cleanse myself of these thoughts!*

As the ceremony concluded and the ship's party headed for their respective stations or to quarters, Emily Morgan approached James Morgan and Captain Bonner. With appropriate pause for reverential mention of the now-departed John Smith, she quickly explained her own proposition. She wished to take a new name. With both her family mentor and a ship's captain at hand, she explained, this should be a good time to perform the necessary ceremony. Within minutes, Emily Morgan formally became Emily D. West. And the event, along with John Smith's untimely demise and burial at sea, was duly recorded in the ship's log.

Favoring currents and wind had moved the schooner to a position 30 miles south-southeast of Cape Hatteras. All appeared to be smooth sailing on to Charleston, with the unfortunate Smith incident now concluded. But as he chewed hard on one of his always-unlit Cubano's, James Morgan concerned himself in quiet thought: *How, with their best contact and most reliable purveyor, John Smith departed from this earthly remain, would the party get provisions.*

His reflections were rudely shattered by a shout from the lookout high in the rigging. "Ahoy below! Ship astern sir...'bout 4 mile north'n west and closin' fast. Could be a sloop o' war. But looks she's flyin' a red flag!"

Lafitte-era pirates favored sloops and corvettes. With 20 or fewer guns, very shallow draft and incredible speed and maneuverability, the larger sloops were the most feared raiding craft along the Atlantic and Gulf coast. A "sloop o' war," technically a corvette, was smaller and lighter than a sloop, with fewer guns and crew, but was even faster than the larger sloop. Almost nothing afloat could outrun it, and a corvette rarely ran aground in shallow coastal waters. Pirates manning any of these vessels flew either the black skull flag (*no crossbones*), or a plain black or red ensign. All had the same meaning...*surrender now or die! Maybe - die anyway.*

Morgan thought that *if the pirates boarded the Flash, Emily West would be the most valuable commodity to be taken, other than the keg of rum, the cannon and its ammunition. At least she'd be the only person from the Flash left alive when the attack was over.* He refused to allow that to happen without a fight to the death, and, stuffing his half-chewed cigar into an open pocket, he pleaded with Captain Bonner to turn the *Flash* 180 degrees - directly into the approach of the raider.

Reluctantly, after ordering his crew below, Captain Bonner quickly took the helm and brought the *Flash* about, facing the pirate ship almost head on. *This, at least, might surprise the raider and provide a smaller target. Significantly it would allow the recoil from the cannon to be absorbed in the long direction of the ship - steadier shooting. And they would now have the wind to their advantage.* As Morgan had hoped and expected, almost simultaneously the crew of the pirate vessel then brought their ship quickly abeam to firing position, and a warning shot echoed menacingly as it crackled past the bow of the *Flash* and struck in its wake a hundred yards aft. Immediately a raiding party was seen descending over the side to longboats and beginning to row hard into the wind toward the rapidly approaching *Flash*.

When the raiding party got within two hundred yards of their bow, Morgan, de Zavala, and West, racing forward, quickly positioned the barrel of the now-exposed 18 pounder slightly above the keel of the raider, alongside and parallel to the bowsprit, aiming at what now was clearly a corvette flying the dreaded red flag. Morgan sighted down the cannon barrel, which he had quietly pre-loaded, and touched off the powder.

FLOOM>>> The ball from his first shot whined toward the pirate corvette, but passed just above the bow, its impact with the sea appearing well over a hundred yards to the east. Morgan hastily lowered the barrel and ordered Emily West to take over the aim as he and de Zavala reloaded. Before the startled corvette crew realized they had indeed been engaged in open sea combat by a common schooner - wet swab, powder, wad, ball, wad, light...*FLOOM>>>* West fired, and the second ball from the *Flash* this time slammed into the hull, splintering her oak into a spray of wood, and leaving a yawning opening in the keel just at the water line. Wet swab, powder, wad, ball, wad, light, **FLOOM>>>** Another ball hammered into the keel near the first hit, expanding the damage. Now water was pouring into the hapless corvette. Emily West and her "distinguished" gun crew had been superb.

The pirate gunners launched two hastily aimed rounds as the corvette turned tail, the projectiles missing high and wide to port of the *Flash*. The raiding party had seen the hits on their now-retreating corvette and reversed course, *knowing that they must join all hands below deck to bail and patch the hull until the ship could be brought to port for repairs. Otherwise, they could sink in a matter of hours, with no rescue imminent for marauders such as them. One way or another their fate was probably already sealed. The Lafitte era code of death by marooning would be their lot for mission failure. If their captain did his job, they'd all die together on some remote island over the next several winter months.*

A shaken but grateful Captain Bonner now hurriedly brought the *Flash* right full rudder. Picking up the current, the ship was quickly south bound once again. *Rather than take the time to sail east beyond the Hatteras sand bars and risk another confrontation, he gambled that their 10 foot draft could clear the approaching sand bars...and it did.*

Captain Morgan reckoned that *the pirate ship would get to shore, probably at Nags Head, where it could be dry-docked and quickly repaired. He knew that when repairs were made, the ship would be hastily but fully re-provisioned and, with a new crew, head east of the Hatteras sand bars. As soon as it could safely clear, it would turn right full rudder, hoist all sails and bear due south for the tip of Florida without stopping. If it could beat the Flash to Florida or the Keys while Morgan and his entourage were docked in Charleston or Jacksonville for further provisioning, it would lie in wait...and when the Flash finally appeared, there would be hell to pay. Could the Flash find protection somehow?*

Day seven put the *Flash* into Charleston harbor without

further mishap. The city was alive, bustling literally with taverns, hotels, pleasure houses and shops. Some displayed the world's finest wares, for those who could afford them. Others provided a selection of provisions for expeditions unequalled on the Eastern seaboard. But prices were high, service was slow and suppliers favored those who best greased their palms. Morgan wanted none of this - *he had no intention of letting anyone enjoy the Old World atmosphere and pleasures of Charleston. In fact his goal was to be resupplied and out of the harbor in less than 24 hours.*

~

Charleston, South Carolina, named after King Charles II, was chosen early on by its planners to be a port city. It was among the ten largest cities in the US in the 1830s and one of the few cities in the original 13 colonies that openly tolerated multiple religious orders and provided at least modest recognition of blacks and other minorities among its citizens.

The invention of the cotton gin by Eli Whitney in 1793 had revolutionized cotton production, and it quickly displaced rice as South Carolina's major export. But the invention of a mechanical cotton processor also guaranteed the strengthening of the Southern slave trade. Cotton plantations relied heavily on slave labor, and slaves were also the primary labor force in and around Charleston in other industries. By 1820, the population had grown to 23,000, with more blacks than whites or Asians. The slave trade itself depended on the port of Charleston, where slave ships could be unloaded and the captives then sold at markets.

~

The words and quiet melody of the most famous religious hymn of the time wafted across the quiet water as the *Flash* tied up at Charleston, near the confluence of the Ashley and Cooper Rivers flowing into the Atlantic. It was twilight on Saturday, and the Christian population of the black community had begun their celebration of the day of rest.

"Amazing grace, how sweet the sound that saved a wretch like me! I once was lost but now I'm found, was blind but now I see."

"Amazing Grace," by Englishman John Newton, a former agnostic slave trader and ship captain, was written after his conversion to Christianity. Newton's life was spared during a violent storm at sea while ferrying slaves from West Africa to the Americas. His story was almost as well-known as his hymn, and both were widely known in every slave community in the new world. As the newly dubbed Emily D. West stood at the railing and listened to the music, *she recalled learning the hymn when she was a young girl at Monticello.*

Despite having only read about Charleston earlier in books, West *felt a particular attraction to the city* - in a word - *freer.* Much of the citizenry appeared to be of mixed-race, and she felt that she was *an instant kindred spirit.* She rightly suspected that *her heritage was quite similar to theirs.* Common gossip of that time held that local plantation owners' wives knew the white father of every mulatto child in Charleston, except those in their own household.

The *Flash's* crew remained below deck under lock and key. Morgan and Bonner knew that *if they let them ashore on a Saturday night, they could encounter privateers and pirate crews in almost any taverns that they frequented. No point risking the crew telling hostile ears of the Flash's recent exploits. Would they also tell that there was a young mulatto woman aboard who was as smart and shrewd as she was beautiful? Probably.* So it was decided that Lorenzo de Zavala and Captain Bonner would remain on board to secure the ship and restrain the randy and idle crew. Only after the ship was being loaded and readied to sail, would they be loosed to resume their duties aboard the ship. They could all have their fun when the *Flash* made port in New Orleans.

Although Morgan considered leaving West aboard the ship too, to eliminate the risk of her being kidnapped, he decided she must accompany him. Morgan first thought that *he and West would go ashore and engage locals that John Smith had told him about in the business community, asking their help to re-provision the schooner. He realized, however, that if he entered the dock area on a Saturday night with this beautiful mulatto, he could easily be overwhelmed and she kidnapped, raped, and sold at auction.*

Now that John Smith was dead and gone, and his Charleston provisioning contacts unknown or useless, Morgan believed that *his only option was to follow West's idea of enlisting the black community's help in restocking the Flash. The young woman had proven herself.* Morgan was confident *that she could present their mission and needs to those who might listen in a way that would persuade some, at least, to cooperate.* So Morgan agreed to Emily West's somewhat risky proposal - reiterating to her the mandate that the *Flash* had to be loaded and away by dawn with whatever they could procure.

~

Even in the black neighborhoods, West's striking presence attracted a crowd. After several inquiries, she and Morgan arrived at the modest home of Nipper and Sarah Grigsby, a well-respected, middle-aged black couple who appeared to represent the community. Morgan let West explain their overall mission and present their request for assistance. They needed stores for 10 days for seven passengers and a crew of five. And they required better defensive weapons. What Morgan sought included water, cured meat, eggs, flour, corn meal, bread, sugar, coffee, rum, six 18-pounders, small arms, ammunition and black powder.

All needed to be loaded on the *Flash* so they could depart before dawn. They would pay well in gold, one hundred dollars, for such a tall order.

The couple conferred and then advised Captain Morgan that West would be the only person they would deal with. "The cannon and small arms would indeed be difficult if not impossible to provide," the Grigsbys flatly stated.

While they could ensure West's safety in the black community, that assurance would not extend to Morgan. He must return to the ship, with his gold, and await her arrival and that of their porters. Morgan protested audibly as he stepped hesitantly out the cottage door, drawing stares from the Grigsby's and others who had gathered outside. West took his arm, leading him through the crowd, as she assured Morgan that she could take care of herself. *He should return to the Flash as instructed.*

Reluctantly, Morgan left Emily West with Nipper and Sarah Grigsby, and a sizeable contingent of blacks, making his way back to the docks. Once aboard the Flash, he briefed de Zavala and Captain Bonner on events ashore, brought the crew on deck for their orders and waited nervously for whatever was to happen.

Their wait was short. Morgan, on the lookout, heard footsteps and whispers along the darkened pier. It was West and the Grigsby's, followed by a train of men in single file, bringing what appeared to be the needed stores. They were loaded within an hour as all hands strained and sweated, but hove to, securing welcome supplies. But only limited weaponry had been provided - several pistols, two long rifles and a 12-pound cannon - along with ammunition and one keg of black powder.

With the *Flash* ready to cast off, The Grigsbys approached Captain Morgan to determine Emily West's status, thinking they could negotiate to make her a freeperson. "Miss West is already a freeperson, but she has a one-year contract with me that is some months from being satisfied," Morgan explained. His words fell on deaf ears. Though he began to count out the $100 in gold for the stores and their services, the Grigsbys firmly refused to accept it. Finally all agreed that the stores they provided would purchase and fulfill the young indentured servant's remaining contract, allowing her now to be a partner, if she wished, in his enterprise. West was ecstatic at this most unexpected turn of events as Morgan agreed cautiously to the demands. But she noted that *no written contract had been made.*

With the supply issues resolved and the deck finally clear of visitors, two of the crew cast off the lines and scrambled aboard *as a slight breeze* Morgan sensed *caught the sails. It would be much better with the ship well out of the harbor on open seas.* Dawn was just beginning to break as Morgan, his ever-present cigar in hand, now felt the ship move, *but backward?* Looking astern, he saw two large flatboats, each rowed by four black men. Lines had quietly been attached to the *Flash* astern, and the boats were towing the vessel noiselessly out of the harbor. When the *Flash* was sufficiently adrift, and its canvasses firmly caught the sea breeze, they dropped the lines, and the flatboat occupants made for shore.

The *Flash* now was moving under its own sail power. The crew on deck resumed their duties. West, de Zavala, and Morgan would take turns on watch. Emily West, now free, had earned the honor of the first watch.

~

This same morning on the Outer Banks near Nags Head, North Carolina, Captain Renato Beluche and his protégé Pierre Crump paced their makeshift dry dock where a corvette that had flown the Beluche flag as a deliberate guise was under extensive repairs. Her crew had let themselves come under fire and be beaten off by the *Flash*, a common cargo and passenger sloop carrying but a single cannon, something that would never happen to a Beluche fleet craft. *It most certainly would not have happened in this situation because a Lafitte or Beluche ship had never attacked, nor would it attack, an*

American flagged ship, Beluche mused to himself.

He ordered Crump to take the crew some 20 miles offshore to a small island and leave them with three days rations, one pistol, 5 balls of ammunition and one tin of powder - *no more* - an action tantamount to slow death. The captain who had brought the crippled ship into Nags Head, *hoping for repairs,* now faced his own demise ashore. Under Beluche's interrogation he had at first been stoic, revealing nothing of the encounter nor his base or true owner, but his punishment had been devised precisely to give the rogue captain an *honorable* opportunity to reveal the true identity of the owner and port of call of the ship. Moments before a gull plucked the first eyeball from his sweat-soaked, bleeding face, the screaming captain had finally yielded the information to Beluche, *in the vain hope that his life might be spared.*

Portions of the captain's lacerated skin and skeleton still hung inside a rusty, iron cage, the entire apparatus suspended on a makeshift tripod. The unmistakable stench of death wafted inland on a light sea breeze. Sea birds picked at the remaining flesh and sinew while Renato Beluche, nearby, considered *what he should do next.*

Nags Head locals were mainly pirates or "wreckers," men (and women) who, unlike pirates rarely sailed, but hung lanterns around donkeys' and horses' necks on shore at night to lure ships aground in the shallows where they could then plunder them. *Thence,* some thought *came the island's name,* "*Nags Head.*" Beluche, a pirate with little use for the local wreckers and their ilk, had served with the Lafitte brothers, Jean and Pierre, for several years, raiding along the profitable eastern shores, as well as in the Caribbean Sea and his native Gulf of Mexico. *He knew these waters like the back of his hand.*

Born and raised in New Orleans, Captain Beluche considered himself to be *a fair and disciplined taskmaster, even a patriot of sorts. He admired the service that he, with Lafitte had rendered to Andrew Jackson and his staff at the Battle of New Orleans and recalled his part in the operation, running guns and supplies from Lafitte's island headquarters in Barataria in support of the eventual American defeat of the British.* Lafitte's services had proved so valuable that Jackson had personally pardoned him and later merely looked on as Lafitte became the virtual dictator of Galveston Island. Though not pardoned along with Lafitte, other events had favored Captain Beluche. He might soon sail from North America to join Simon Bolivar in the fight for South American independence.

This day, however, Captain Beluche had resolved that *as soon as the damaged corvette was seaworthy, he would take this ship that had illegally flown his flag and attacked an American vessel, return it to its port of call, and confront its owner. For that mission and his later voyage, if he survived, he'd need 10 of his best men and provisions for perhaps a month at sea.*

If the opportunity presented itself, Beluche further thought, *he would also personally inform the captain of the Flash and its occupants that it was not a Beluche ship they had encountered.*

Chapter Six

November 1834

The *Flash,* her passengers and crew now more seasoned and watchful, enjoyed a relatively uneventful transit between Charleston and Jacksonville. James Morgan and Captain Bonner were still concerned that the reappearance of the pirate corvette or one of her sister ships might wreak havoc at any moment, but there were no ship sightings of any consequence by the time they reached their first Florida port. The weather had been particularly mild, and the waters had been calm since that first violent storm near Hatteras, and most aboard had settled into routines for the long journey around the Keys and on to New Orleans and Texas. If all continued to go as planned, the party might reach New Washington around Christmas time.

Emily West increasingly found her attentions focused on Lorenzo de Zavala. Their chance morning encounters, their evening lingering around the mess table after Captains Morgan and Bonner had excused themselves - even occasional brushes against one another in the ship's narrow passageways left the young woman feeling more romantic than ever before. *Indeed de Zavala was much her senior, maybe as old as James Morgan, but there the similarity with Morgan, or any other man previously in her life, ended. What was his real history? He'd almost certainly enjoyed the comfort and intimate companionship of beautiful women in his life, and was now apparently married to the woman who'd been with him at Captain Morgan's mansion. But now she was in Paris and de Zavala was here on the Flash with her. He was charming without guile - attentive without imposing. He was ruggedly handsome - well educated. A man of the world, he seemingly embraced power without being addicted to it. Was she in love or just infatuated? No answer - Emily West simply knew there was a mutual attraction that, one day would be consummated if she had anything to say in the matter.*

The *Flash* made port in the Florida Keys on 12th November. After conferring with Captain Bonner, Morgan and de Zavala decided to give the crew and passengers three days of much-needed rest ashore before proceeding west across the Gulf of Mexico toward New Orleans. Morgan reasoned that *any encounter with their earlier attackers would have already occurred.* Bonner agreed - although neither knew the real identity of their attackers.

Key West, settled more than three hundred years earlier, was Florida's largest city. The Spanish had named it "Cayo Hueso" - Bone Island, recognizing its history of death from shipwrecks, disease and other misfortunes, both natural and manmade, over the years. With English mispronunciation, Cayo Hueso eventually became "Key West."

Because of its natural deep water port, then the largest on the east coast south of Norfolk, the city was home to American naval facilities, ship salvage operations - wreckers - and occasionally, to pirates as well. The sizeable ship salvage and wrecking industry had spawned taverns, hotels and other far less savory attractions. In fact in 1834 Key West had more taverns and brothels per capita than any other North American city of the time. Whites made up more than 500 of the 700 inhabitants. Most were professionals - doctors, engineers, naval architects - others were shopkeepers, fishermen, wreckers and provisioners, catering to the myriad sailing ships traversing the mid-Atlantic, Caribbean and Gulf. The rest of the population was about evenly split between freed blacks and slaves.

Morgan, de Zavala, Captain Bonner and Emily West took lodging at a hotel at Front and Duval Streets, near the wharf where the *Flash* had docked. Captain Bonner and his crew had been given the list of provisions and the necessary contacts from Morgan so that this time they could have a more orderly and complete provisioning for the next run - from Key West to New Orleans. Along with better armament for the *Flash*, the list called for the recruitment of at least three qualified gunners willing to engage unfriendlies on the high seas. Bonner busied himself with organizing his short stay in Key West to be certain the ship was ready and that he had reconnoitered what he remembered to be the less-traversed passages through or around the two most dangerous reefs - Carysford and Crocker.

~

Only days before the arrival of the Morgan party in Key West a messenger had approached Dr. Henry Perrine, a prominent city physician, in the tropical herb garden behind his residence with a message that his friend and former professional associate, Lorenzo de Zavala y Saenz, would arrive in port at the latest on the following Friday. Perrine, former US consul to Mexico, had started an experimental planting and herbal medicine operation, the Tropical Plant Company, in Key West after departing the diplomatic corps. Sisal, one of Dr. Perrine's experimental plants would eventually play a pivotal role in the development of the southeastern US. At the moment though, Perrine was one all too familiar with the US conflict with Mexico as well as with de Zavala's passion for addressing the problem. So he was eager to help the cause of the New Washington Association in any way he might.

Dr. Perrine invited the Morgan party to a gala dinner at the family compound, ostensibly to discuss the progress of the New Washington Association and its needs. Perrine had advised de Zavala earlier in a message delivered to his hotel, that several other like-minded guests and their wives would be in attendance. Among the guests would be Dr. Benjamin Strobel, local Army chief surgeon, well respected in the community. And there would be Jacob Houseman, perhaps the most successful and best-known ship salvage expert on the entire East coast. Both Strobel and Houseman were quite influential, not only in South Florida, but also in the efforts to expand US influence in the West. Dr.Strobel had ideas to further the efforts to curb disease and illness, as well as contacts for medical supplies and doctors in the West.

Houseman lent his considerable wealth and influence as a purveyor of goods and services, shipping and transport. But unlike Strobel, Houseman's somewhat unsavory reputation in some circles had preceded him. Some said that *his salvage operation was nothing more than legalized shipwrecking. And rumors persisted of his slave running, now illegal in Florida, and his dealings with known pirates to purposely ground cargo vessels for salvage. One of Houseman's reputed tactics,* according to the now-deceased John Smith, *was to engage fishermen to remove or relocate navigational markers warning of shallows so cargo vessels could be purposely grounded for plunder.* After disputes with the courts in Key West some years earlier, Houseman had suspiciously bought and developed nearby Indian Key as an independent base of operations, inheriting with the purchase a general store, hotel and 9-pin bowling alley.

Knowing the nature of the dinner guests, particularly Houseman, de Zavala approached Morgan with the proposal that Emily West should accompany the party, perhaps posing as his wife. As he described to Morgan, *de Zavala was convinced that Houseman would likely have knowledge of any pirate activity in the Key West area, and Emily West was the one person most likely to charm that information out of him.* Morgan reluctantly agreed, *already suspecting a more personal motive on de Zavala's part for including West.*

The dinner party was a sumptuous affair. Fresh conch, snapper and a variety of other sea delicacies were served, along with rice and beans - staples of coastal life from Charleston around the Keys and on to Texas. There was ample French wine and local ale for those who wished to imbibe. Jacob Houseman ate and drank perhaps more than his share, earning him increasingly harsh eye contact from his wife, who was sitting to De Zavala's right.

Seated next to Houseman, Emily West sipped at her glass of Chateau Lafite 1818, *remembering Mama Hemings'*

stories of how Jefferson in Paris had owned several fine late-1700 era
vintages from this same winemaker. Jefferson had been prudent to
conceal them behind a false wall in a nearby restaurant cellar during
the French Revolution. Fortunately while president he had then been
able to finally retrieve them from Paris and store the lot at
Monticello. Wine had been a source of great pleasure for Jefferson,
but she'd never pilfered even a sip as long as she lived under his roof.

"Señora de Zavala I understand you have experience in
hotel and dining management. Captain Morgan tells me that
you will run the hotel he is constructing in New Washington,
no?" Emily West's reverie had been interrupted by the
gravelly voice of Jacob Houseman. He was leaning in toward
West, lightly touching her arm - a bit closer than polite
conversation called for, and he had spoken in passable
Spanish. West responded in kind. Her Spanish with practice
now had a particularly Castillian lisp, uncharacteristic of
Mexico. And her demeanor was sufficiently arrogant to back
Houseman away to a sociable distance. "Yes Señor
Houseman. If fortune smiles on us and we encounter no more
pirates or other hazards of the high seas, we should be in
business early in the new year. I understand you also are a
hotelier and restauranteur?" Houseman responded, "Most
certainly, Señora, and I would be pleased to show you my
properties should you wish."

"Unfortunately our time does not permit such a visit,"
West responded then went on, "I am told we must sail soon.
However another matter, Señor Houseman," this time West
surprisingly grasped his arm as she spoke. "I am to
understand that in your other businesses, you may have
knowledge of persons wishing to hinder our progress -
perhaps to further their black market commerce?"

Houseman was shocked *almost to sobriety* by West's
touch and her pointed, blunt query. At the same time he was
also taken by her regal, yet intimate demeanor. He seemed
compelled to respond. "Señora de Zavala, I am informed that
two men were in my establishment recently in Indian Key
inquiring as to the schooner, *Flash*, and her party. I had no

idea until tonight that this vessel was one affiliated with the New Washington effort. I know these men sparingly, but their captain is well known. Renato Beluche is from the old Lafitte organization. My information is that he has two well-outfitted corvettes, flying no flag, now docked at Indian Key. Though it appears they seek revenge for some past encounter with the *Flash*, I have no interest in their plans, nor will I assist them. I shall see to it that they cause you no ill. You have my word."

Before West could respond, the attention of the diners turned toward Dr.Strobel who had noisily launched a boisterous recounting of colorful stories about his time spent hunting for rare birds on the island with the naturalist, John Audubon. Strobel's talk was enhanced by a series of apparently original Audubon sketches that he produced from a leather pouch at the side of his chair. But West, still concentrating on the comments from Houseman, knew *she must deliver the information regarding the pirate corvettes to de Zavala and Morgan as quickly as possible. She had little faith that Houseman would indeed be their protector, simply in the interest of Texas' future independence. They needed to get out of the Keys as quickly as the Flash could be provisioned.*

Not surprisingly the notoriously unstable fall climate of the Florida Keys soon brought about another arrival of foul weather. Flashes of lightning, and close by, almost simultaneously, artillery-like thunder cracks interrupted the Perrine dinner party. After hasty expressions of gratitude to their host, the guests were soon scurrying for their drivers and carriages, buffeted by sheets of rain blown horizontally by tropical wind gusts.

Once in their carriage and bound for the hotel, a rain-soaked West informed an equally drenched James Morgan and Lorenzo de Zavala of her dinner conversation with Houseman. Morgan chewed hard on his damp cigar. "Damn it all! If Beluche and his crews are already in the Keys, there is little chance that the *Flash* can make it to New Washington unchallenged. Even if Beluche lets the *Flash* get to New Orleans and take on provisions, as soon as we sail into open gulf waters and turn west toward Texas, he'll attack from Lafitte's old stronghold in Barataria Bay."

Morgan feared *that the men aboard the Flash could be killed if they did not desert, and that West would be taken by Beluche. The provisions, and, perhaps even the Flash itself would be given to the crew of the corvettes so they could pillage other ships in typical Lafitte fashion. Morgan must,* he thought, *now mull over his options, however scant, overnight. He would then inform West, de Zavala, and Bonner of his decision.* Complicating matters further was the deteriorating weather, typical of the season in the South Atlantic and Caribbean waters.

~

West's room was on the first floor at the rear of the hallway near a storage area, remote by intent. Still dripping and chilled, she slipped the key into the lock and opened the door, then turned to close and secure it. West was looking forward *only to dry nightclothes and warm bed covers.* Tomorrow was another day. But before she could secure the entry, an almost spectral form appeared from the shadows, clamped a rough hand across her mouth, wrapped a strong, wet sleeve and arm around her waist and wrestled her to the floor. To no avail West struggled to reach the knife in her boot.

"Madame de Zavala - or West, or whomever you actually may be, I will remove my hand and myself from you only on your oath not to scream or try to attack me until I can tell you my reason for being here. You are a beautiful woman, but I am not here to take advantage of you in any way." Captain Renato Beluche announced all this in a low, but convincing voice and with no menace in his tone. He too had been soaked in the downpour.

"Who are you and what do you want? I do not know you!" West shouted in response, hoping perhaps that, *despite Beluche's warning, de Zavala or Morgan would hear her and investigate the commotion.*

"Madame you must lower your voice if we are to continue a civil encounter! My apologies for such an intrusion and for my appearance. I am Captain Renato Beluche, and I have little doubt that my character has been maligned tonight by a certain Jacob Houseman of your acquaintance. Yes I am as some say - a pirate - and may be guilty of many sins, but attacking an American ship is not one of them. I know Mr. Houseman personally and I know that he, in fact, owns the ship that attacked yours near Nag's Head. Further, as a deliberate ruse, he instructed his captain to fly an ensign similar to the Beluche flag during this attack and earlier ones. His attack on the *Flash* was repelled, I understand, by your gunner who fired two shots from an 18-pounder amidships? If this is true, it is a humiliation that Houseman must certainly address. Otherwise, his seafaring dominance, his reputation, and particularly that of his illicit raiders, is ruined."

Beluche now loosened his grip on West, allowing her to sit up on the floor. She spoke calmly. "Mr. Houseman's story contradicts yours in its entirety. He said that you owned the ship that attacked us near Nag's Head. He said that you were docked with two raiders at Indian Key and that your intentions were to sink the *Flash* and kill the captain and crew as retribution. So why should I now believe you instead?"

"His captain made a confession to me shortly before he died," Beluche replied.

"And of course there was no coercion?" came West's sardonic response as she added, "Your friend Mr. Houseman suggested that we might get a visit from you tonight,"

"One expects such chicanery from him. Mr. Houseman is unquestionably quite mad and greedy - but quite clever," Beluche replied. "Never have I had any intentions of harming the *Flash* or any other American ship. We would not even consider it! I am a patriot - a supporter of the revolution, of Andrew Jackson and now of the New Washington movement against Mexico. I am likewise in league with Simon Bolivar and other patriots of the Americas in their revolutionary efforts against European oppressors - Spain in particular!"

Now quite angry and animated, Beluche continued, "I will most certainly call on Mister Houseman tonight to see that the matter is settled between myself and him as to the Nag's Head incident!"

West realized too late *that her quick implication of Houseman had sent Beluche almost into a fit of rage.* He stumbled out of West's room and through the empty hotel lobby. Beluche was *livid* as he made his way through the village streets and up the long approach path to Houseman's guest quarters in Key West. He pounded the door, which, after a delay seemingly of minutes, was finally opened cautiously by Houseman, wearing rumpled bedclothes - a nightcap covering his sparse pate and gripping a candle in hand.

"Captain Beluche, what in God's name are you doing here in the middle of the night? Are you in pain - injured? What is wrong? You are white as a ghost!"

"Most certainly I am injured, you treacherous bastard! That woman aboard the *Flash* who claims to be Zavala's wife has just confirmed the lies you spread tonight as to one of MY ships attacking the *Flash*. I am at my end with you and your duplicities. You will never again misrepresent your own piracy as mine!" Beluche responded harshly.

"Please, I do not know what you are talking about. This woman that you refer to must be lying. I've had no talk with any such woman. I have not said anything about a ship of yours attacking a ship called the *Flash* or any other ship. Come in - we shall have a drink and settle this amicably," Houseman said, reaching for Beluche's arm.

"You Mr. Houseman are hardly worth the cost of the powder and ball required to dispatch you," Beluche rasped, almost in a whisper, as he cocked and aimed a mahogany-handled flintlock directly at Houseman's head. "Out the door now - we are going for a short walk on the beach. There you will permit me to introduce you to your Maker."

Terrified and pleading, Houseman, barefooted, in his nightclothes and still holding the extinguished candlestick, was shoved out the door and down a rain-slick stone pathway toward the incoming tide, ever returning to the deep abyss of the sea.

~

Doctors Perrine and Strobel and Constable Nathan Wilson were summoned when Houseman's barefoot, still-clothed but seawater soaked body was found by two fishermen at daybreak. It had drifted near the dock at the rear of the Houseman guest quarters. A severe bruise, with embedded sand, seaweed, and other debris, indicated that Houseman had probably fallen and struck his head on a large stone somewhere near the path to the beach. The blow had apparently caused him to lose consciousness and drown at high tide. His distraught wife stood nearby. *Why had he been out here? Did it have something to do with that de Zavala woman he was talking to at dinner last night?*

The constable quietly addressed the new widow. "Mrs. Houseman, my sympathies on your husband's most untimely demise, but I must ask you a few questions." Mrs. Houseman nodded stoically. "From all appearances, Mr. Houseman has died from a most unfortunate accident on the beach. Do you have any reason to doubt this? Do you know of anyone who would have had animosity toward your husband to a degree that would lead to such bloodshed? Were there any unusual events or noises at your guest residence last evening? "

"My husband and I have not shared a bed for many years, I regret to say, and I heard nothing from my bedroom. Many were the times I'm sure he entertained late night visitors. He was a shrewd, successful businessman, and I am sure that in this and other places there were many who would be glad to hear of his demise," replied Mrs. Houseman. "To your question however, I know of no specific reason that someone would want to harm my husband. Let me hasten to add that my husband admonished me early in our marriage not to get involved in nor to question him as to his businesses."

"Mrs. Houseman, I thank you for your patience and courtesy in answering my questions at such a terrible time," the constable stated. "Your husband was a very prominent person in our community, and throughout the east coast, for that matter. It is my responsibility to fully investigate the circumstances surrounding his death. However it would seem that Mr. Houseman's death was due to some event - an accident without foul play. Even so I am most grieved by your loss."

~

Morgan, de Zavala, Bonner, and West were at breakfast in the hotel dining room when Doctor Perrine and Constable Wilson entered and informed them of Houseman's death. "There are several unusual matters to clear up regarding events of last evening," stated the Constable as the Morgan party sat in silent disbelief.

Constable Wilson: "Gentlemen and Señora de Zavala, I know that Mr. and Mrs. Houseman were at Doctor Perrine's last night. Did any of you see him after you left Doctor Perrine's or hear anything suspicious?"

"No Constable. We returned to the hotel together, had a short meeting, and went to bed because we require an early departure for New Orleans this morning," responded de Zavala. Morgan then queried the captain of the *Flash*. "Captain Bonner, any thoughts about Houseman's possible enemies?"

"None, sir," Bonner replied in support, though as a sailor he'd heard the stories - more than rumors, about Houseman's pirating and wrecking connections.

Throughout the Constable's and Dr. Perrine's visit, West kept silent and no one queried her directly - but she already knew the truth. *And perhaps they all knew the real nature of Houseman's demise, as well?*

"So our New Washington endeavor has lost another strong backer in Jacob Houseman. We could certainly have used his funds and influence," Morgan lamented. "I only wish it had been Renato Beluche, instead."

"And why is that, Captain Morgan?" asked a surprised Constable Wilson.

"The *Flash* was under attack and about to be boarded several weeks ago by a pirate ship near Nag's Head when we fired on the ship at close range. Our aggressive action caught the captain and crew by surprise, and the ship sustained substantial damage. I am sure it required a dry dock for repairs. We learned just last night from Mr. Houseman that the ship had indeed been repaired and, along with a companion craft, was now moored at Indian Key, with Beluche and his crews no doubt preparing to attack the *Flash* in retribution," Morgan replied.

"Captain Morgan, surely your party misunderstood Mr. Houseman," countered Constable Wilson. "Admittedly a pirate to some, I assure you Captain Beluche prides himself, as did the Lafitte brothers under whom he sailed, on being American patriots. To my certain understanding, they have never fired on or otherwise attacked an American flagged ship. By God, they all sided with Jackson at New Orleans. Not only would Beluche not attack the *Flash* - if you had asked, he likely would have required one of his ships to escort you the way to New Washington to see that no harm befalls."

Pondering the significance of the constable's remarks, Morgan responded, "Constable, thank you very much. The thought of someone like Captain Beluche, as a patriot and perhaps as our benefactor in this instance, is difficult to imagine. But your insight is indeed thought-provoking and already brings considerable relief to me. If there is anything that we can do to assist, please let us know. Otherwise, we would like to sail as quickly as possible to try now to get ahead of any more weather."

"Please proceed at your convenience, Captain Morgan," Constable Wilson advised. "It appears rather obvious to me that this was an accidental drowning, perhaps precipitated by an unfortunate fall. And as we locals also know, Mr. Houseman was a man who liked his drink."

~

Constable Wilson and Dr. Perrine took their leave as West and de Zavala made their way through the hotel lobby to their rooms. Morgan was summoned to the front desk momentarily to pick up a message left for him earlier. He read the unsigned note, *puzzling over the party's apparent good fortune.* The message was short, but specific and written with a quality instrument. "The provisions you require shall be waiting in the main storage warehouse adjacent to the east pier at 2 o'clock today. Please accept them for aid in your just cause." It was unsigned and carried the closing sentiment, "With the grateful respect of all who are protected by our Patron Saint, Brendan the Navigator."

Morgan was dumbfounded. *Could their provisions be from Renato Beluche – or from associates of John Houseman? Both were mariners.* Though Morgan knew that *the saint was said to be the guardian of navies and sailors, did this belief and its perceived protection extend to wreckers and common pirates? Whatever the source, if provisions were indeed available, at this point he was happy to have them. It was time to get out of Florida and on to the Gulf.*

The crew of the *Flash* worked through the afternoon and into the evening to load the provisions. This time, in addition to foodstuffs, there were scores of small arms and crates of ammunition that Morgan and de Zavala knew *would be quite useful when they finally reached Texas.*

Foul weather was blowing in again on the Florida Keys. Lightning and distant thunder announced yet another squall line approaching. Lines were hastily cast off and the *Flash* moved into the Gulf to get quickly on the leeward side of the islands, her course set for the mouth of the Mississippi River and on to New Orleans. At the same time two corvettes, now flying the true Beluche flag, quietly slipped their moorings at Indian Key. One, via provisioning calls in St. Dominique and Cuba, then bypassing Aruba, was sailing for a distant and troubled Venezuela. The other, as ordered, protectively shadowed an American-flagged schooner en route to New Orleans.

Chapter Seven

New Orleans, founded by the French in 1718, named in honor of the Regent of France, Philip II, Duke of Orleans and sold to the US by the French in 1803 as part of the Louisiana Purchase, was already noted for its cosmopolitan, yet diverse, population and mixture of cultures. This land acquisition, Thomas Jefferson's crowning achievement, effectively doubled the size of the fledgling United States. The population center, New Orleans, had grown rapidly too - with Americans, Africans, French, and Creoles steadily taking up residence throughout the 1830s. The muddy Mississippi River and docks at New Orleans teemed with watercraft - more steamers and flatboats than ocean-going sail-driven vessels. New Orleans had wealth and regional influence as the largest gulf port. And this largest city in the South retained a bawdy, frontier town atmosphere, despite its continental influence, wealth and charm.

The *Flash*'s port call in New Orleans promised to be a restful one for Morgan, de Zavala, and West, who took lodging at la Maison Montblanc, a small, luxuriously appointed mansion in the French Quarter. The crew, under the supervision of Captain Bonner, busied themselves on the dock loading provisions to take them finally on to New Washington. As for Morgan he had business to attend with local officials that took him away for the first day and early evening. He had tendered for a second ship, the *Kosiusko*, to take additional personnel and supplies to New Washington and he needed to finalize the transaction.

A soft but insistent knock at West's door awakened her from a restful sleep at mid-morning. "Who is there?" she addressed the bolted door warily.

A doorman replied, "Madame West, Señor de Zavala requests the pleasure of your company in the hotel dining room if you are so disposed."

"Yes, you will please inform Señor de Zavala that I accept his invitation and will be there within the hour." As a person of mixed race West had *no concern with being seen alone with a Hispanic man in a dining room in New Orleans. This was a city of diverse cultures, and usually no questions were asked.* She dressed quickly and left her long hair to its own arrangement, her heart now pounding as she stepped into the dining room. A waiter eyed her discretely, taking her to de Zavala's back corner table, where a bottle of chilled Dom Perignon sat, ready to be uncorked and served. Lorenzo de Zavala smiled, rising from his seat as she approached.

"Señor de Zavala, thank you for the invitation. And such a lovely beverage - you must know my innermost wishes."

"It is my pleasure, Miss West. I would call you Emily, but I can only do so if we toast a closer relationship and you agree to address me as Lorenzo."

As de Zavala helped West to take a seat next to him, she arranged her skirt and responded. "Señor de Zavala, we have spent time together on the ship, but little private time. So first please tell me more about yourself. You are obviously a learned man, an entrepreneur, and as well, an able diplomat and politician. What about your earlier years? What about your family?"

De Zavala, also now seated, sighed deeply, took a sip from his champagne flute and then spoke. "I was born in 1788 in Yucatán, New Spain. I graduated from the seminary at Mérida in 1807, after studying French, English and Latin. It was then that I entered the newspaper business and editorially began to express my views about politics, morality and democratic ideals. Unfortunately my views clashed with those in power in the land and led to my imprisonment in Vera Cruz in 1814. I studied medical textbooks while in prison and was prepared to practice medicine when I was finally released in 1817. However, in 1820, I was elected to public office, and in 1821 was appointed Deputy to the Spanish Court in Madrid. Due to my interest in politics, my career in medicine was short-lived.

"I had married Teresa Correa in 1807 after graduation from seminary. We had two children. Regrettably my wife died not so long ago, in the spring of 1831. After her death, I spent several months in France and England, and then decided to live in New York City. My children, now three, reside at this moment in Paris with my new spouse."

At this point, West recalled aloud de Zavala's visit to the Morgan Mansion with his fiancée, remembering her as attractive but somewhat cold and reserved. She also commented to de Zavala on the similarity of their names.

"Correct, my dear. That was Captain Morgan's dinner party in Philadelphia in honor of Mssrs. Alex de Tocqueville and Gustave de Beaumont in October 1831. My new fiancée and I had the privilege of an invitation to that affair. We were greeted at the door by a darkly beautiful young woman - with shining black hair and blue-green eyes. She spoke fluent French and Spanish. I recall thinking 'how striking, how is it that she is from the Morgan household, is she spoken for?' However, I had already become engaged in the fall in New York after I returned from Europe, and we were to be married just a month after the dinner party. Ah, and another matter - I must also now say I was most surprised when you, after John Smith's death aboard the *Flash*, petitioned Captain Morgan to change your family name to West. As you were aware, 'Emilia West' was my fiancée's maiden name. Quite a coincidence - no? Or could this act have had some deeper purpose? I have always wondered?"

West appeared to take this unusual fact into consideration without any real surprise or change of demeanor. She made no response *other than a half-smile* as she asked de Zavala to continue.

"Politics in Mexico intervened and I left New York for my troubled homeland in 1832, but without my fiancée. She remained in New York while I served as governor of the State of México, and in Congress as a deputy for the state of Yucatán. In 1833, President Santa Anna again asked me to serve as minister to France, which I gladly accepted. Emilia and my children accompanied me. However, I quickly learned after arriving in Paris that Santa Anna had assumed dictatorial powers. I denounced his actions, resigned my commission, and returned to New York City - Santa Anna had warned me not to return to Mexico City. My new spouse and my three children are still in Paris. I plan to relocate them to a new Texas "republic" after Captain Morgan and I discharge our current obligations to the New Washington Association.

"So, Señorita Emily Morgan West, that perhaps in too much detail, is the story of my life. Now to yours?"

As Emily West shifted positions in her chair, she began. "Much briefer and less intriguing I would say, my dear Señor de Zavala. I am told I was born in 1811 in New Haven, Connecticut. My family name was Miller - the daughter presumably of a white father named Miller and a black mother - not uncommon these days. But my earliest recollections are only of the Jefferson household at Monticello." *Now for the first time West was able to speak openly to someone about her life at Monticello, the incident with John Smith and how she had come into the service of James Morgan. Telling the story to de Zavala, she felt the weight of keeping such secrets lifted, and de Zavala appeared to be as totally enthralled with her background as with her beauty and poise.* As West finished describing the events in her life, de Zavala broke in. "You do not mention marriage. Are you spoken for? Is there a man in your life?"

As she sipped her second glass of champagne, West responded, somewhat flirtatiously now, in excellent Spanish. "Thanks to you my dear Señor, I was Señora Lorenzo de Zavala for a brief period at Dr. Perrine's dinner party in Key West. Does that matter? If so, it would suggest there are now in fact two Señora Emily, *(or is it Emilia?)*, West de Zavalas - one in Paris and one here in The New World."

"Regrettably the marriage to a most charming Emily West, now in my presence, was not consummated," de Zavala sighed convincingly and responded to the flirtation.

"However, as a former minister to France, learned, even qualified, in matters of matrimony in both France and Mexico, and knowing the Catholic laws and liberal customs of the city of New Orleans, surely I am authorized to accomplish such a consummation."

"A very tempting offer, Minister de Zavala. Who knows what might happen to a woman's inhibitions in this fine hotel after such a morning repast and charming conversation with a learned gentleman? May I have another flute of Dom Perignon perhaps?" Emily West leaned closer and took de Zavala's arm. She slipped her hand into his open sleeve.

~

Much later they lay exhausted, side-by-side on the bed in de Zavala's suite - the bedcovers now partly covering their spent and still-naked bodies. As pleasurable as the experience with de Zavala had been, Emily West now became pensive, *one day this will amount to no more than memories of sexual needs fulfilled. We can never grow old together.* Meanwhile at her side de Zavala slept deeply without thought or dreaming.

The next morning while Captain Morgan and Lorenzo de Zavala were still in their rooms, West browsed the French Quarter looking for a more accessible defensive weapon. She did not ever want to be as vulnerable as she had been in her room that night in Key West with the pirate, Renato Beluche. Finally she found the perfect piece - a five-inch double-edged, razor-sharp knife and lightweight scabbard that could be concealed in the top of her stocking at mid-thigh above the outside of her right knee. The knife was the latest design - a self-locking, spring-actuated switchblade from Chatellerault of France, recognizable by its s-shaped cross guard and engraved ivory handles. It was not cheap, but its mechanism and quality were unquestionable - *a dependable defense*, she thought.

The *Flash*'s trip back down the Mississippi was accomplished with ease. With favorable current and wind, it took half the time it had taken to sail up the river. The ship entered the gulf at South Pass and headed for Galveston, a distance of roughly 400 miles. The *Flash* would stay within 35 miles of the coast. Barely an hour after the ship passed Barataria Bay, Captain Crump again eased in behind, just out of sight over the horizon. He was following Beluche's order to never again allow the *Flash* to sail unprotected in American coastal waters.

The *Flash* approached Galveston four days later. A day after their brief port call in Galveston, they anchored in San Jacinto Bay, just offshore from New Washington where piers and dockside warehouses we're still being constructed. West and de Zavala had been in proximity often, but discretion and formality were the order of the day.

Chapter Eight

May 1835

"Emily, you, Señor de Zavala and I have made much progress in the months since we arrived last December. Completing the layout of New Washington, and developing this establishment at what some of my associates are now calling Morgan's Point has been my highest priority. You have learned quickly the frontier ways and been instrumental I would say in organizing the hotel and staff. Learning to manage the hotel and restaurant business, I readily admit, required new skills to those of running the house in Philadelphia, but you have performed without flaw. Recently, however, you seem pre-occupied. Is there something that troubles you?" Captain Morgan asked.

"Captain, I knew before we left Philadelphia that Sally Hemings's health was declining. For whatever reason she and her children are the closest to family that I've ever had, with all respect to your kindnesses. In a recent post from her son, Eston, in Charlottesville, he advised that she continues to falter. I fear it is some kind of consumption or a related malady. And she may have passed already. I have no idea - I have not seen my Mama Hemings since I left Monticello almost 10 years ago. If it's possible I am compelled to see her one more time before she dies." West went on, "I have a proposal to present to you that might allow me to do so. Would you have time to discuss it, perhaps after you dine tonight?"

"You may do so now, if you are ready," Morgan replied.

"I am, sir. I know that regardless of whatever verbal arrangement you made with the Grigsbys back in Charleston regarding my freedom, I am still legally under contract to you as an indentured servant through December of this year, and I know that my compensation is $100 per year, or about $2 per week. I have studied maps and talked to Captain Bonner. I know that it would take approximately six weeks for me to get from New Washington to Charlottesville, a week to visit my mother, and six weeks to return to New Washington. This assumes that I could sail to Norfolk on the return journey of the *Flash*. If so, I could then make my way to Charlottesville and back to Norfolk in time to board ship to return to Texas. I have enough money to travel between Norfolk and Charlottesville, but not enough to pay for my passage between New Washington and Norfolk.

You would be without my services for some 13 weeks or more, which is one-fourth of my contract. My proposal to you is this - if you will allow me leave for this time and arrange for me to sail on the *Flash* - when I return, I will work the remainder of the year for room and board only. And I will enter into a contract with you for an additional year as an indentured servant at $75 per year. This should provide $50 for my sailing expenses."

Morgan responded, "You have obviously given this plan considerable thought. While I believe that you owe no such debt to Sally Hemings, I nevertheless understand your loyalty to her and to our deceased President Jefferson. I would not permit your attendance at his rites, but it is only proper that I now give you leave and cover your sailing expenses as you propose. My only wish is that Señor de Zavala or I could accompany you. I don't like the idea of you traveling alone.

Regrettably I simply do not have the time to do so right now, and Señor de Zavala is in the midst of the construction of his house on the San Jacinto River. He plans to move his wife and children from Paris soon. In fact it's possible they could be on the *Flash* as it returns in the Fall. And there is much more that he needs to attend to with me and with his Texas governmental affairs. So, suffice it to say your proposal is acceptable to me, with your promise to be at the service of Captain Bonner and to accept his protection."

"I promise to do so, sir, because I am excited about returning to New Washington," West replied. "This is my new challenge and my real opportunity for a future."

Morgan and West began to plan West's trip in detail. Again he expressed concern about her safety and stressed that she must maintain the papers certifying her contract as an indentured servant. He provided a letter certifying that West had his permission to travel to and from Charlottesville. Otherwise, she could be at risk whenever she went ashore at various ports of call. Captain Bonner was assigned the responsibility of seeing that West was properly attended when the *Flash* was docked at Key West, Charleston, and Norfolk. Bonner and the *Flash* would continue on to Baltimore, Philadelphia, and New York City after West disembarked at Norfolk. West would take the steamship James from Norfolk to Hopewell and on to Richmond via the James River. From there, she would take a stagecoach to Charlottesville along the Three Notch'd Road, an established, if rough, east-west route across central Virginia. The total distance from Norfolk to Charlottesville was roughly 200 miles and would take at least three days after she disembarked from the *Flash*. *This would be the riskiest part of the journey,* Morgan believed.

The *Flash* sailed from its new dock at Morgan's Point in early August. Bonner and Morgan finally agreed that sufficient provisions could be loaded so that stops at New Orleans or Pensacola would not be needed. Key West would be the first port of call.

The *Flash* again ventured no more than 35 miles off the coast as it sailed from the Mississippi delta to Key West and maintained an even closer shore route as it progressed along the east coast to Charleston and on to Norfolk. Unknown to its occupants and crew, the *Flash* was again shadowed by one of the pirate Beluche's corvettes and her crew, captained by Pierre Crump. Bristling with 18 pounders they once more obeyed their sworn agreement to guard the *Flash* from any hostile acts on the high seas.

At one point early in the transit to Key West, all aboard the *Flash* were alerted by the ominous sound of cannon fire, well to their rear and out of sight of the lookout. Whatever conflict had ensued appeared to have been brief, however, and all concerns eased after a few anxious hours of watchful attention to the vacant horizon. Some 25 nautical miles astern Captain Crump's corvette had put three 18-pound balls midships of a coastal raider, handily splintering it and dispatching the two, almost separated halves to a watery grave. No rounds had been fired from the hostile vessel. In their boarding craft Crump's crew had picked up any remaining hands from the sunken sloop, slit their throats and returned them to the gulf waters - leaving a trail of blood for hungry sharks and other predators. The remainder of West's journey to Norfolk aboard the *Flash* was uneventful.

As James Morgan had ordered, Captain Bonner introduced West to the captain of the steamship *James*. They showed him her papers and assured him that West had James Morgan's permission to travel alone. Her papers found in order, West made the remaining journey to Richmond without incident.

West's stagecoach ride from Richmond to Charlottesville began uneventfully. She kept to herself and had no conversations with the other three passengers - all of whom had consented to riding with someone of mixed-race in advance. However, at the first rest stop some 30 miles outside of Richmond, the driver, a young, sullied white man, approached West as the other passengers entered the wayside inn. She'd seen his type before - ill-fitting clothes, unkempt hair under a sweat-stained wide-brimmed hat, a small chin and hooked nose above a mouth showing crooked, yellowing teeth. He spoke. "Ya' know ya' ain't allowed inside wih them white folks. Now…I ain't never had no mulatto on my coach before. And a damn fine looking one y'are, at that - all lonely too, I reckon? Why don't you and me make this trip a little more enjoyable for both us? Nobody's gonna be th' wiser fer it. Let's have a quick screw in th' coach 'fore you go in th' back to pee."

West ignored his remarks.

"I asked you a question, nigger woman!"

"Very well, to your improper question and quite rude remarks, the answer is 'no.' Now leave me to my business."

"I can surely leave you alone and you can do yer 'bizness'...back out there with th' rabbits n' cuy-otes." He waved his hand in the direction of the wooded hillside next to the inn. "Yep, I can leave yore ass alone right here and let you fight fer yourself. Y'er probably a runaway, anyway. If you goin' to get so damn uppity, maybe I just better have a look at your papers. See who you belong to." The driver reached for West's embroidered handbag as she pulled away.

"My papers are fine. They were reviewed and I was approved to travel by your agent at the Overland station in Richmond," she replied calmly.

"Well, that agent ain't driving this damn stage, now is he? What's the matter with you, anyway? Why're you in such a foul mood? Is yore 'fe-male time' upon you? That don't bother me none. C'mon now!" The driver reached out again - this time for West's arm.

West wrenched deftly away from his grip. Feigning a stumble, she quickly reached through the slit in the folds of the right side of her skirt, slipping the switchblade knife she had purchased in New Orleans from its scabbard. It made a distinctive metallic click that seized the driver's attention as the blade locked into place, and West gripped him firmly by the collar. She raised her now-armed hand quickly and touched the knife to his throat. "Maybe this WILL bother you," West whispered into his hat-bent ear.

With both hands above his head, the driver anxiously responded, "Oh shit, lady - hey, I didn't mean no o-fense. I just thought you might want to, you know...where'd you git a nut cutter like that? Why all you people always gotta have them knives?"

Shoving him away, West said loudly, "Our conversation I would say is finished and we have an understanding. The only thing I want to know from you is how quickly you can get your skinny ass up in that seat and take me to Charlottesville to see my family?"

The driver glared but turned on his heel and went into the tavern. "ALL ABOARD, FOLKS, bound for Charlottesville!! Let's get a move on." West went to relieve herself while the other three passengers re-boarded. Finished, she then boarded the coach in silence.

~

Charlottesville had been home to two U.S. presidents, Thomas Jefferson and James Monroe. These men had also served as governor of Virginia, living in Charlottesville and travelling to and from Richmond along the Three Notch'd Road, the same road that West had just been down.

"Hello, Mama Hemings," West said quietly as she stuck her head in Sally Hemings' bedroom door. Her surrogate mother lived in the house behind the one owned and occupied by her son, Eston, on Main Street in Charlottesville. "Do you know who this is?"

"Oh, my baby Emily," said Sally, looking up with a smile on her frail face. "It's my baby girl. How are you, my child? I was so afraid that I would pass before I could see you again. Sit here by me and tell me all about yourself. What have you been doing? Has Captain Morgan been good to you? Do you still live in Philadelphia? Are you married? Do you have children? What brings you to Charlottesville? How did you get here? How long can you stay?" Sally Hemings stifled a wheezing cough.

"So many questions, Mama Hemings! Too much talking for you. First things first - you bring me to Charlottesville. I wanted to see you. I wanted to hold your hands. I can stay some days yet, but I do have much to do in the new western territories where I am now with the Morgan party.

"Now let's talk about you. Eston and Julia tell me that you've been ill, and I see you're still in bed - and with a serious cough. What can I do to help?"

'Oh, honey, I feel as good as I'm gonna feel. The doctor says that I have consumption, and all he can recommend is bed rest and fresh air. I saw so many people die from consumption when we lived in Paris many years ago - 'cause there were no medicines to cure it then - and there are none to cure it now. Your coming to see me is the best medicine any doctor could prescribe." Sally Hemings heaved, her chest rattling now from one of her uncontrollable coughing spells.

"I was so glad when I heard you had come to Charlottesville and were living with Eston and Julia, Mama Hemings, because I knew they would take good care of you. I was very concerned about how you would cope when you left Monticello," West said.

"You were concerned! Baby, was scared to death! I had not had to fend for myself since I was 15 years old. Mr. Jefferson's will provided for Madison, Eston, and me to finally be freed. Madison and Eston moved to Charlottesville right after Mr. Jefferson's death, but the family asked that I remain at Monticello for a time to help with some...well, let's say delicate matters in the will. Then I moved to Charlottesville to the first house here that Eston built for him and me." A deep cough and Hemings continued, "Eston and Madison put the training they got at Monticello to good use by starting their business in carpentry and woodworking. They're well known for their work and stay very busy. Eston built a house on Main Street when he married Julia in 1832 and built me this house behind his house. Best thing was we didn't have a lot of money worries, thanks to those 'delicate matters' with the Jefferson's at Monticello."

Her breathing was labored now, but Hemings doggedly continued. "Julia's father was a Jewish merchant, and her mother was of mixed-race, just like us, so we got along fine. Still do. Julia got pregnant late last year. Until I took to this bed, I mostly looked after the baby, did the cooking and housekeeping while Julia helped Eston and Madison in their work. But I just don't have the strength to help with anything anymore. It will only get worse."

"Mama Hemings, please don't think that. The bed rest and fresh air have just got to help. And maybe the doctor will find some new medicine to help," chided West.

"No sweetheart, our days on this earth are numbered and mine are comin' to their end. I thank the good Lord for the many blessings that He's bestowed on me. But for God's Grace, do you realize that all of us could be living in a shack on a cotton plantation, pickin' all day and feedin' that noisy Whitney gin all night - still slaves to some plantation owner?" Another deep cough and rattling echoed through Hemings' chest.

Her voice now more hoarse and growing weak, she went on. "Oh, I've heard the snide remarks that people made about me being Tom Jefferson's 'yellow Monticello whore' and livin' in sin. Well, they can just kiss my ass!" A short laugh prompted still another coughing spell. "All my life in Monticello's none of their concern. Tom Jefferson and I never shared a bed while he was married. He idolized Mrs. Jefferson and was never unfaithful to her. He was broken-hearted when she died and promised her that he would never remarry. As far as white folks care - he never did."

Hemings continued, her chest heaving now more noticeably, "If they only knew. Mrs. Jefferson's father, Mr. Wayles - he was also my father. That's just the truth now, baby. We were half-sisters. Mrs. Jefferson's mother died a time after giving birth to her and Mr. Wayles married two more times, with both wives dyin' on him. After the death of his third wife, Mr. Wayles and my mother became intimate - they had six children. But my mother never shared a bed with Mr. Wayles while he was married. When Mr. Wayles died, mother and we children became the property of Mr. and Mrs. Jefferson and we moved to Monticello. Mother lived there until she died many years ago.

"I have lived a charmed life, my child, since I was 15 years old – all due to dear Tom Jefferson. I have visited England, lived in Paris, traveled through Europe, and spent weekends at villas in the south of France. Ahh, I do miss Provence. To the bigots who say that I should not have lived the life I lived and had the relationship I had with my Tom, I say, 'and do what? Work myself to death on a cotton plantation with two hundred other nameless, faceless black folks?' I thank the Lord everyday for my blessings, and I have to ask Him, and only Him, to forgive my sins. I will continue to do that till the day I die, which is not going to be long coming.

"Now too much about me, my dear, and I'm too weak to go on jabbering anyway. Tell me about you. How did you get to Charlottesville? You shouldn't be traveling alone. Is someone with you? Where are you going when you leave here? Do you need Madison or Eston to go with you?"

"Mama Hemings, you don't need to concern yourself about me. I can take care of myself. I had a very good teacher growing up. When I leave here, I'll go back to Norfolk and board a ship bound for Texas. That's where I now live. I work for Captain Morgan in his hotel and restaurant business in New Washington, and I am so excited about my prospects. Even though we are not yet part of the United States, Texas is a great country itself. My hope is that we won't be part of Mexico too much longer. I feel free there...freer than I've ever been, and Captain Morgan has been extremely kind to me. But I agree with you that I, too, could be living on a plantation and picking cotton, were it not for God's blessing.

"Why don't we get some rest now? My bottom is tired from riding a stagecoach for a day and a half, and I know you are tired. All that coughing and wheezing takes the gumption out of you. I am going to sleep right here on a pallet next to you, so you call me if you need anything. When we wake up in the morning, we will take up right where we left off."

"I will, my baby, I will."

Sally Hemings died in her sleep that night - *quietly, gloriously happy!*

~

Meanwhile only a few days after West had departed from Morgan's Point, nearly half-way around the world, Emilia West de Zavala and de Zavala's three small children traveled by first-class coach from Paris to le Havre, on the northwest coast of France, then boarded a ship and set sail to Baltimore. She and her husband, Lorenzo de Zavala, had made the trip over from New York City years before with two small children, but that route was shorter and she had had help with the children. She knew that *this trip would be a more arduous one with three children, no help, and a longer route taking approximately six weeks, depending on the wind and weather. Plus, many of the 160 passengers were German emigrants - inordinately rowdy and immodestly promiscuous. The crew of 20 would be kept busy.* Madame de Zavala would be, as well, *on guard to limit what the two older children heard and saw.*

And what further culture shock our children will experience upon our return to America, de Zavala thought. *Leaving the pristine setting of their Paris villa, under the virtually full-time care of their 35 year-old, educated French nanny, and sailing for six weeks on a ship loaded with rowdy Germans - then boarding a small schooner to sail another six weeks to the Wild West - Texas territory - with no telling what kind of low life. This is not what I envisioned when I married Lorenzo de Zavala four years ago in New York City. My return to Texas - perhaps even the Unites States, may be brief.*

Baltimore lay west-southwest of le Havre. The ship's course, however, started out almost due south. When they reached the Azores, they picked up favorable trade winds that brought them across the Atlantic, along the coast of North Carolina, and on to Baltimore in a northerly direction - a relatively uneventful sailing.

Such a sight for sore eyes, Emilia de Zavala thought wearily as, 39 days after leaving France, they made port in Baltimore. Fort McHenry, an elegantly designed stronghold, it's battlements forming a pentagon-shaped perimeter, loomed over a bustling harbor scene. The fort had served its city and country well in battle since 1798 and as recently as 1814. After the US declared war against England in 1812, the British had burned the Capitol Building and the White House in Washington, and then set their sights on capturing and controlling Baltimore and its harbor, one of the busiest on the east coast. Baltimore was one of the targets in a three-pronged maritime attack that included controlling the St. Lawrence Seaway and New Orleans. The British aim was a complete sea blockade of the fledgling democracy to force it into recognition of the king once again.

A combination of regular US troops and volunteers at Fort McHenry had withstood a withering all night cannon and rocket barrage from British warships and had later repelled a land invasion by British troops from aboard the ships. Captain James Morgan had been part of that land battle and had distinguished himself in the fight by stubbornly holding one flank, but at considerable cost to his infantry unit. The same night and into early morning, Francis Scott Key, an American lawyer aboard a British warship in the harbor negotiating a prisoner exchange, was inspired to pen his poem, "The Defense of Fort McHenry." Key was later to serve as the attorney for Tennessee congressman, Sam Houston, in his 1832 impeachment trial before the US House of Representatives. Ever short of temper and lacking patience for "fools," Sam Houston had brawled with another congressman over a trivial piece of legislation. Houston was acquitted but resigned anyway.

Fort McHenry now flew two flags. At the top, the garrison flag with 23 stars and 13 stripes - below - *"that star spangled banner,"* the one Key had seen from the harbor. This was a flag with 15 stars and 15 stripes - flown over the fort in 1814, and a reminder now to a pensive Emilia de Zavala of *the successful defense of the city and harbor.*

In his letter, Lorenzo de Zavala had advised his wife that the trip from Baltimore to New Washington could take another six weeks. With the exception of the short break they would enjoy in a hotel near the harbor, and perhaps one more en-route, Emilia de Zavala realized that *by the time she and the children got to New Washington, they would have been at sea for three months.*

Chapter Nine

Summer and Fall 1835

West was sitting on her luggage, patiently waiting as the *Flash* negotiated its way to the pier and tied up at Norfolk.

"Bonjour, mon capitaine. Est-ce navire par la voile chance de New Washington, du Texas?"

"And a good day to ya, as well, Miss Emily West," Captain Bonner replied..but in his Scottish-laden English. "Th' *Flash* is indeed bound fer New Washington and there's 'ready a berth set f'r you alone."

"Thank you, Captain Bonner," West smiled. "It is so good to see you again."

"Your stepmother'n, family must be doing better fer such a display a' good spirits from ya," Captain Bonner responded.

"She is doing fine, Captain. She is in Heaven. And the rest of my family can now get on with their lives, as all of us must too. I am happy to return to New Washington."

"Aiee, my condolences, Miss West. T'is most regrettable - t'is indeed."

"Thank you, Captain. But I am very blessed that I got to see her and hold her one more time. She was my friend, my inspiration and my idol. No one like her will walk this earth again."

Emilia de Zavala was still on deck near the gangway when the striking, raven-haired, bronze-skinned woman boarded the ship at Norfolk with a salutation in French to the captain. Her greenish blue eyes, though cold, sparkled when she spoke. *What brings an attractive, mixed-race young woman who speaks fluent French and who obviously knows the captain well to board this ship at this backwoods hamlet of a port - and what requires her to sail to New Washington? And why do I already have some innate dislike of her? Jealousy? Mistrust? Why? I KNOW I've seen her before - maybe years ago. But that young girl, no -*

woman - was in the Morgan household, and her name was not West, was it??

After West went to her quarters, Emilia de Zavala paced the deck until Captain Bonner acknowledged her presence. "Good afternoon, Captain. I trust that there is not a problem that has required us to dock at this place."

"Oh no, Ma'am de Zavala," Bonner replied. "T'was a scheduled stop a' Norfolk to pick up Miz' Emily West, in th' employ of Cap'n James Morgan, the man who owns this ship. Aye, we dropped Miz' West off now some weeks ago a' way up to New York City. She'll be sailing wi' us back to New Washington."

"Interesting," de Zavala said. "Just what does this woman West do for Captain Morgan? Is she a housekeeper?"

"Aye, an' much more than that, ma'am. She's managed domestic affairs at Cap'n Morgan's home in Philadelphia fer several years. When Cap'n Morgan and your husband decided to go to New Washington last November, they took 'er with 'em fer they knew she'd make th' excellent hotel and restaurant proprietor fer 'em in New Washington."

Emilia de Zavala continued her questioning of Captain Bonner,"What was she doing in Norfolk?"

"Family's been ill in Charlottesville so Cap'n Morgan gave 'er leave to go see to 'em. 'Er Mama, 'er somebody she calls 'Mama' at least, passed shortly after she got there last week."

"How kind of Captain Morgan to allow a domestic such liberty," de Zavala noted. "She must be very special."

"And that she is, ma'am. She is a very bright one and tough as they come on th' frontier."

"I overheard her salutation to you in French when she boarded. When it is convenient to do so, you should please have her meet me. We must have matters in common in our past."

"T'would be my pleasure, Ma'am - soon as possible. I'd planned 'er a'ready." Bonner touched the tip of his cap bill in respect as he turned back to his duties.

76

The *Flash* eased out of her moorings in Norfolk and turned south, as the newly introduced Emilia West de Zavala and Emily West leaned, side-by-side, against the port railing. The excited de Zavala children peeked out from the folds of their mother's skirt at the coastline and at their mother's new acquaintance. At one point Emilia de Zavala thought *she detected the unmistakable scent of a fine cologne or eau de parfum - lavender and lilac, maybe jasmine, from Grasse en Provence - coming from West. The fragrance was her husband's favorite during their time in Paris, but she herself disliked such tanner's smells, as she called them.* Both women now silently entertained their own private thoughts on their mutual object of affection - *Lorenzo de Zavala and when they would see him next.*

~

As the *Flash* plied the coastal waters of the Atlantic, more than a thousand miles to the west, David Crockett stepped onto the porch of his small cabin near Rutherford in West Tennessee. At least thirty well-armed volunteers were waiting on horseback and in heavily loaded wagons in the open area in front of the cabin. The sun was just casting its first rays through the mist rising out of the cotton fields to the east, promising another hot, sweltering day for field hands. Despite the heat, Crockett wore his usual leathers, but no coonskin bush cap. *That frankly was an affectation pushed on him by the many stories and stage plays making the rounds in the East these days.*

David Crockett's crossed arms cradled a long rifle, *his favorite*, given to him in Philadelphia some years earlier by an admirer of his politics - Captain James Morgan. Crockett spoke. "Boys th' time's come fer us to help ar' friends in Texas. Mexicans and Spaniards think they kin have all that land fer themselves. It ain't gonna happen. Besides, all us here could like life in Texas ourselves when we finish runnin' 'em off. Land here'n Tennessee's goin' fer a dollar-ten a acre. In th' Texas territory - why it's less'n ten cents! My family, 'specially daughter, Matilda here's jus' itchin' fer me to come git 'em when we're done with Henerale San 'tana." Then responding to cheers and shouts of agreement, Crockett stepped off the porch, waved to his wife and daughter and headed for Jackson, *to round up more volunteers* he hoped, in Madison County before ferrying west across the Mississippi at Memphis and on to meet with Houston in Arkansas.

~

Some weeks later, in the hill country of central Arkansas, Sam Houston sat beside a smoldering campfire outside a Cherokee Indian lodge and smoked his pipe. Years earlier, back in the eastern Tennessee mountains after Houston's unhappy, self-imposed departure from Congress, the Cherokee had made him an honorary member of their tribe and given him the name *"Connoheh"* (the Raven). When the Cherokee were forcibly resettled, Houston had fought the decision as hard as he dared, in the end resolving *to accompany most of them on their "trail of tears" to their new reservation.*

Sam Houston loved his life with these Indians. He had taken a half-Cherokee mistress - a young widow, Tiana Gentry. And though the Cherokee recognized the two as married under their customs, Houston *still agonized over his unconsummated, but legal marriage, some years back to Eliza Allen in Gallatin, Tennessee. What a mistake - taking on Eliza and her father - a close confidant of Andrew Jackson. He'd been so embarrassed by all the falderal, he'd resigned as Tennessee governor and later high-tailed it for these hills of Arkansas. Jackson, he was told, was still furious with him!*

But in all, Sam Houston's life was good at the moment. His trading post on the Verdigris River, *"Wigwam Neosho"* was flourishing. He was respected as an elder in the Cherokee Nation. *Politicians and politics back in Tennessee could go to the devil.* At the moment, though, Sam Houston had only a restless peace within himself. *David Crockett and a sizeable contingent of men and supplies had passed through heading west a* few weeks earlier, bringing with them more news of the fight brewing with Mexico and maybe Spain for control of Texas Territory and beyond. Arkansas Territory bordered on Texas, and there were strong indications that matters along the Rio Grande were badly out of hand. Crockett had had maybe 50 to 60 men with him when he passed through on his way to New Washington - not nearly enough to make a real difference, Houston thought. The new Republic of Texas, if that's what it was going to be, needed a leader - and a real army to stand against the Mexican juggernaut! Crockett had said as much himself and had urged Houston to come with them.

Since then Houston had even tried through his old Congressional contacts to get authorization from the Commissioner of Indian Affairs and the president to lead the Cherokee Nation into Texas territory in support of the Tejanos and Texians. President Andrew Jackson however would have none of it - not wishing to "further damage relations with Mexico by permitting armed savages to fight for the US." Houston privately suspected the rejection was more personal and wondered if matters might be more favorable, had the first presidential assassination attempt - by Richard Lawrence last January - been successful. And the irony in that incident was that both David Crockett, still in Congress at the time, and Andrew Jackson had been able to wrestle the deranged man to the ground when both his pistols had misfired.

Houston would have already left for Texas, but *Tiana wasn't coming.* Houston remembered *their painful talks, his useless pleadings, as she put it.* No, Tiana would never live in Texas or anywhere west of where she'd already been forced to come to. She missed the hills of Tennessee. Well, to hell with that, Houston fumed to himself, *Tiana or no Tiana, I'm off to Texas!*

Chapter Ten

December 1835

Nothing was settled about the future of Texas in and around the embattled enclave of San Antonio de Béxar this day, 14th December. The city with its old mission and military garrison was situated strategically along the San Antonio River and astride major trading routes in all directions. The central government in Mexico had early on recognized its political and military value, designating San Antonio de Béxar as the seat of government in the northern territory - Coahuila y Tejas. By the time of the siege by Texians, the town had about 1,600 residents - mostly Tejanos, Mexican nationals and Béxarenos - comingled families of the original Spanish aristocrats from the Canary Islands who had been given land grants to Béxar in the 1700s by the King of Spain.

Earlier in November General Santa Anna had received the dire news from his staff at his headquarters encampment in Northern Mexico. His own brother-in-law, General Martin Perfecto de Cos and his garrison at Béxar, was being besieged and starved out by a band of 700 Texians under command of Steven Austin. At one point during an evening lull in the siege, the Texian troops were visited by their new commander, Major General Sam Houston. After the evening mess, outside on a damp, chilly evening, Houston spoke to the assembled troops on the need for Texas never to agree to a truce and remain part of Mexico. *This would gain them no support elsewhere in the world.* "Rather," he said, "We must declare our full and unconditional independence from Santa Anna's tyranny and the influence of Spain. Thus we may insure the support not only of the rest of America, but allies abroad, as well." Houston's stirring words inspired the Texians to complete their rout of General Cos' force and send his Mexican troops in full, muddy retreat southward.

Santa Anna now saw his task clearly. He needed to put a stop to this madness on the part of his rebellious Tejas Territory - he must destroy Sam Houston and his "volunteer army" or drive them permanently back across the Mississippi. *Who was this Anglo intruder, this general, who had just come to Texas? If Houston was a great general, why hadn't Santa Anna heard of him or read of his exploits?* So on Santa Anna's orders over just a few weeks, his own army near San Luis Potosi swelled to almost 6,000 well-trained and seasoned infantry, horse troops and artillery. Their ensuing winter march northward late in 1835 through the Mexican desert, and its often, mountainous terrain, was brutal. It was the worst winter that had ever been recorded in that region, and Santa Anna's army suffered hundreds of casualties. But their forced trek - with the general always close at hand through, snow, rain and incessant mud - would bring them into Texas territory months before Steven Austin, Sam Houston and others expected. They were pressing due north toward San Antonio and the Alamo garrison. Their mission? To avenge the fall of Béxar!

The Texian army, on the other hand, began to suffer desertions, leadership bickering and lack of equipment and organized resupply. Local politicians blamed Sam Houston who, though he appeared every inch the seasoned soldier, was to some of them *not the dynamic leader and brilliant military strategist from Tennessee whose scrappy, aggressive reputation had preceded him.* The internal politics emanating from conferences at Washington-on-the-Brazos further complicated the uncertain situation. Endless debates between the War Party and the Peace Party saw local representatives take uncompromising stances – sometimes even involving local militias. From Houston's perspective *there were now way too many cooks in the kitchen, and if he could prevent it, they wouldn't be allowed to spoil dinner. He wasn't leaving, but he needed time to regroup and plan a sound attack strategy.* Houston much preferred *to meet the Mexican Army in the open on his terms at a time of his choosing.*

Meanwhile, Jim Bowie, a strong influence in the Battle of Béxar, went east to New Washington to meet David Crockett and his contingent of volunteers from Tennessee. Other troops from Béxar broke their encampments along the Cibolo River and, though Houston had questioned the wisdom of a fortified, static defense, they had now been garrisoned at the Alamo mission in San Antonio de Béxar.

The conflict with Mexico was entering a more inflammatory stage. Stories spread that the few Texians captured earlier at Béxar were, as Santa Anna's new "give no quarter" mandate directed, shot by firing squads and left tied to improvised railings, or hanged by the neck in trees - their rotting corpses presumably discouraging further insurgency. One or two of the most vocal and aggressive combatants were rumored to have suffered Santa Anna's extreme punishment - "deguello" (beheading) - thus irrevocably inflaming tensions and demands for retribution from Texans, whatever their heritage. Because of the stories spreading of deguello, *Mexicans were now unquestionably considered barbarians.*

~

In New Washington, Emily West busied herself with readying the kitchen and wait staff for the guests who would soon be coming down to dinner. The town and hotel were situated on a small hillock overlooking Morgan's Point, a narrow strip of land and natural harbor where Buffalo Bayou from the west flowed into the San Jacinto River and Bay. New Washington would disappear and in later years, become part of the new town of Houston. But Morgan's Point would survive as a hamlet on its own.

Looking out the window past the flagpole in the small town square, West noted the continuing drizzle and low clouds hanging over the docks and San Jacinto Bay, She felt *as though it had been raining forever.* Adding to her gloom was the fact that since arriving once more on the frontier, she'd had ample time to dwell on the fact that *the de Zavala family was now back together after years of separation - and living, it appeared, quite contentedly in their new house further north on Buffalo Bayou.*

~

The two weathered outdoorsmen had enjoyed an excellent meal in the New Washington Hotel dining room, thanks to Emily West and her hotel staff. The cold rain and mud outside mattered little to them. Jim Bowie smoked a foul-smelling cigar made from local tobacco as he coughed, spat into a kerchief and chased his whiskey shot with another strong ale. David Crockett sat across from him, dressed in heavy woolen trousers, a long coat and shirt, rather than his usual leathers. He was sipping his third ale. They continued their evening conversation, "swapping lies," as West stood in the kitchen doorway, trying to be discreet with her eavesdropping. A fresh-faced, young black man, clad much like Crockett and Bowie, leaned against the door opposite her. He tried vainly to hold her attention, but he was somewhat politely rebuked. *West was not interested in his flirtations.*

Crockett was animated, "Jim, how'd you ever git mixed up with that pirate feller, John La-Feet? I know you t' have more gray matter'n that." Bowie responded, "Aw Davie it was easy. Lafitte was runnin' Galveston tighter'n a bird's ass 'n those days. Nothin' moved he didn't know about. Hell all th' two hundred lived here was personally approved by him 'fore they could come near th' island. But I had what he wanted - or if I didn't, I could find it quick. We did some good bizniss...me an' him - it'uz all 'bove board, I swear - rum, rice, slaves 'n all that. Even Gen'ral Jackson knew what we was doin'. Then one day in comes th' goddam U-nin-ted States Navy! Stopped it all cold, they did. Lafitte left in a hurry. Ah hear tell 'e's gone now - on a island somewhere's - probably dead'n buried."

"Ol' John la-Feet would'na lasted a day where I come from," Crockett responded. "One raid he'd make up th' Tennessee, trying' ta steal a flatboat load'a skins and we'da shot 'is nuts off from 3 hunnert yards."

"You hill folks shore love them long guns. Guess y'all don't like gitt'n them hands bloody. Now us bayou folk favor th' knife," Bowie snarled, almost menacingly, it seemed to the startled West. At the same instant he drew from his shirtwaist a 10-inch long "broad blade" with a distinctive carved blood trench, driving it point-down deep into the tabletop for emphasis.

Emily West approached the table quickly, "Gentlemen there'll be none of that tonight. Texas needs all the able-bodied men she can muster." West knew her clientele. Crockett's heroics as a pioneer and statesman were already legendary. *He was rugged but not handsome,* West thought - *no appeal to her. Bowie had his charm and liked to think he was a ladies' man. Certainly not her type either though - a real bayou brawler. But she did admire his blade and had heard of his exploits in the "Louisiana Sandbar Fight." He'd killed a sheriff there single-handedly, disemboweling him with his knife after being hit twice by pistol balls shot by the sheriff and his deputy. And was Crockett as proficient with a long rifle as people said. There were the stories that Crockett shot squirrels in the eye at two hundred yards. My God,* Emily West thought, *both these boys have drunk too much, and I need sleep.*

Bowie, after one of his increasingly rattling, wheezing coughs, spoke, "Miz Emily we meant no harm. Ah wuz jus' shown' this hill country sharpshooter th' merits of a L'uziana blade. We'll retire to bed now - right, Colonel Crockett?" Bowie patted Crockett affectionately on the shoulder. Nodding agreement, Crockett summoned his aide, the young, black freeman, Henry Baynes Crockett, from the doorway to help him to his quarters. The younger Crockett, who had earlier been standing next to West, trying without success to keep her attentions, now hurried to David Crockett's side. He was completely devoted to the man who had freed him years earlier from an aging West Tennessee cotton plantation owner for fifty dollars, and with Crockett's permission, had taken his last name. Henry had seen good and bad times with Master David and he'd already seen more of the new territories than he'd ever thought he might. But Henry had never, EVER seen *anything... anyone... as beautiful and striking as Emily Morgan West - his secret infatuation - his yellow rose.*

None of the four could have known that December night to what limits their courage and resolve would soon be tested. None would fail their destiny. All would leave an indelible imprint on Texas history and the lore of a new nation.

Chapter Eleven

January 1836

As the proprietor of the New Washington Hotel and Restaurant, West had settled in and picked up where she had left off as the former steward of Morgan's Philadelphia estate, and James Morgan was pleased. West's wide-ranging abilities gave him more time for the New Washington Association. Each morning, while she oversaw the kitchen and wait staff in preparing breakfast for the guests, she also was planning the noon and evening meals, as well as ordering provisions, checking on the chambermaids and running the reception desk area.

Business was brisk and guests varied widely. Two of the best known, Jim Bowie and David Crockett, had been guests for more than two weeks. Bowie had left a few days ago for the Alamo mission at San Antonio de Béxar. David Crockett, along with his ever-present aide and the rest of his Tennesseans, most of whom were camped outside of New Washington, would depart any day now. *Henry Crockett was nice enough when he was around catering to David Crockett's every need,* but West would be glad to see him leave. *He was obviously struck almost speechless in her presence and doted on her every move and comment.*

West had doused the potential dust-up that one evening between Bowie and Crockett, who were both slightly drunk, without incident. She had quickly stepped in and, with some effort, removed the huge knife that Bowie had wedged in the tabletop. Then she had playfully slipped it into a sash around her waist and, with a smile, told Bowie that he could pick it up at breakfast when he had sobered up. Bowie had apologized to her the next morning, telling her to keep the knife, "to keep th' peace on yore premises. I got another one in my kit."

And West had used her bowie knife...quite often, but so far not to draw blood. West's clientele could, on occasion after trying to drink all the ale on the premises, get too boisterous. When they did, she could get their undivided attention with a rap of the bowie knife handle on the table and a touch of its tip gently to her cheek or lips. West would then slip the blade into its scabbard on the belt around her waist. Most tavern patrons got the message and settled down. The one or two that had not, had been escorted out at knifepoint.

Emilia, on the other hand, was not coping well in her new environment. West thought that *she and de Zavala's wife had established at least a mutually respectful relationship on the voyage from Norfolk to Texas, but, if so, it had dissolved upon their arrival in New Washington.* West rarely saw her and the children after the de Zavala family moved into the impressive house that de Zavala had built on a point of land overlooking Buffalo Bayou, near San Jacinto Bay. He had hired (or commandeered) sufficient local staff to prepare meals and to maintain the house and extensive grounds – which he promptly named *"Zavala's Point." After all,* he'd reasoned, *James Morgan had "Morgan's Point," so why not have equal recognition?*

West had heard from her staff the gossip that Emilia's criticism of her servants was relentless, and that Madame de Zavala was an *uncompromising perfectionist* - a poor trait on the frontier where almost nothing was perfect and patience was a virtue. She heard the stories too, that De Zavala's business and political acquaintances and their wives, when entertained by the Zavalas, were *put off by Señora de Zavala's New York and Parisian sophisticate airs. Some wondered how long she could tolerate Texas - and how long Texas would abide her?*

Emilia de Zavala, for her part, was painfully aware that West and her husband saw each other just about every day because, as he repeatedly pointed out when questioned about his many absences - he and James Morgan had common business interests that required his presence at her hotel. *Did the 'common business interests' include French perfume she* wondered, because she could damned well detect the scent of jasmine and other fragrances, particularly when he came home after some of those late night meetings?"

In her frustration, Emilia de Zavala began to develop a plan for dealing with her perceived adversary, Emily West. *Obviously she could not match her beauty - nor was she the promiscuous, raw frontier 'brawler' she thought West to be - traits that, she was certain, would have attracted de Zavala to West in the first place. But West's aggressiveness and organizational skills could be worked against her. At least they could be used to occupy more of her time - keep her away from the hotel and her husband.*

At one of Emilia de Zavala's rare evening dinners with her husband at home, she plied him with one of his favorite wines, had the staff prepare redfish from the bay, fresh pole beans with red peppers from the garden and dismissed the children quickly from the table when dessert was finished. De Zavala knew his wife had a motive for all the attention she lavished on him. *He suspected the worst.*

She spoke. "My dear Lorenzo, we must talk about Miss West." *Now my indiscretions will be aired. Am I ready for this? Is it time to simply confess and send Emilia and the children back east?* But de Zavala was totally unprepared for his wife's next sentence. "She is a bright girl - a bit too pretty for her station in life, but an excellent hotel administrator and logistician. Though I am not fond of that establishment, with its bare wood everywhere and stale smell of ale pervading the place, Miss West keeps the public area and the clientele in good order. As your friend Captain Bonner might say 'aye, she runs a tight ship.'" De Zavala, breathing slightly easier, nervously smiled in agreement - still wondering *where the conversation was going.*

Emilia de Zavala continued. "The last time I had occasion to accompany you to the New Washington Hotel, did you and good Captain Morgan not discuss in some detail the logistics and organizing needed at the new port to properly aid in the defense of Texas?" Once again De Zavala could only nod his agreement. "The two of you wondered aloud how such a difficult task could be accomplished - 'not enough able-bodied men for Houston's army, must less one with sense enough for such a quartermaster's job,' I believe you said? Well why not an able-bodied woman? Give the task to Miss West! She'll be up to it and then some I predict."

De Zavala, *relieved that his infidelities had been passed over, at least for the moment,* was quick to agree with his wife's idea. With little preamble he later the following day presented the plan to James Morgan *who had already harbored similar thoughts.* They summoned West immediately, telling her of the additional duties they planned for her. "Gentlemen," she responded, "I am willing to take on any assignment - well, almost any assignment - if it will aid The New Washington Association and Texas. But all I know about ships is that I have sailed on the *Flash* three times and on the steamboat *James* twice.

"I am as you know experienced in dry goods and food storage and running households and a hotel. That hardly qualifies me to be an army quartermaster or port authority. I have no experience with proper munitions storage and shipment, bills of lading, tidal charts, ship tenders, supervision of a port facility or control of a customs house. With that said, now tell me precisely what you want me to do, what resources I have to do it with, and when you want it done."

De Zavala and Morgan blinked in surprise - possibly with identical realizations. *Tidal charts? Ship tenders? Customs House? We are supposed to be the leaders of the campaign - at least in this area. None of this had occurred to us either.*

Chapter Twelve

February-March 1836

David Crockett and his men left New Washington for San Antonio de Béxar and the Alamo garrison near the end of January. It was still rainy and cold in southeast Texas, and there was deep mud everywhere. Wagons had rutted the roads, making travel of any kind miserable and slow. From the porch of the New Washington hotel, Emily West and James Morgan saw Crockett's contingent off. As usual Captain Morgan was stoic, but West uncharacteristically had tears welling in her eyes. *My God,* she thought, *this is the first time I've cried since Mama Hemings died, and I barely know these men.* West suspected intuitively *that Crockett and his volunteers would never leave the Alamo alive.* As he manned the reins of a supply wagon, Henry Baynes Crockett, himself as anxious and frightened as he'd ever been, noted the tears in West's eyes and thought that *they were shed for him alone.* He too somehow *sensed impending doom.*

Jim Bowie was already at the Alamo garrison, and sharing command with Colonel William Travis. Travis was in charge of the regulars - Bowie, the volunteers. For Crockett's entire march west to San Antonio, his young aide, Henry, wrote in his diary at every opportunity. Around the evening campfire the young black man rarely joined in the conversation, preferring to "keep on scribblin' " as Crockett would say - all the while not permitting any of the party to see his writings. To David Crockett it appeared that *his young freeman was obsessed with maintaining a record of their progress and their travails.*

By late February after several delays enroute, Crockett's forces entered the Alamo. They began setting up their encampment and defenses while Crockett sought out his comrade, Jim Bowie. He found Bowie in his quarters - in bed with a half-empty whiskey bottle and two loaded pistols by his side. His bare knife rested in his belt. "Jim you fool, put that blade on th' table. You liable to roll over on it an' kill yoreself 'fore th' Mexicanos can!" Bowie's response was a long wheezing cough, followed by spitting mightily into the bandana in his hand before he propped himself on his elbow to speak. "Davie, you ole' hillbilly sonofabitch - welcome to el Paridisio de Béxar! Even in th' rain this hill country's prettier than anything you ever saw in Tennessee - other'n a bear's ass or two - you sight'n him down that long rifle barrel." Another violent coughing spell, this time from laughter, left Bowie unable to speak further. Crockett took his leave, nodding acknowledgement to Bowie's aide as he went out – and barely ducking the low door transom. Robert Morales, the aide, a lanky, mixed-race local – a great marksman with a questionable past - merely shook his clean-shaven head side-to-side in exasperated response.

~

Santa Anna's army began arriving in force in early February, the general crossing the flood-swollen Rio Grande on 12th February and arriving at his commandeered headquarters in San Antonio de Béxar on the 23rd. All the while Travis and Bowie sent out scouts and messengers to Houston's command in the east, passing through Mexican lines with only minor skirmishes and few casualties on either side.

Notably although the Alamo defenders, almost to a man, thought *they might be reinforced and somehow prevail*, General Sam Houston did not favor an Alamo defense. He'd consistently stated that he preferred fights in the open to fortified encounters and, at one point in February ordered the mission burned and the defenders to retreat eastward. Travis ignored this order, instead on 24th February penning a brief, eloquent plea for reinforcements:

"...I shall never surrender or retreat. Then I call on you in the name of liberty, of patriotism and everything dear to the American character to come to our aid with all possible dispatch. VICTORY OR DEATH."

The same evening that Colonel Travis wrote those words, Henry Baynes Crockett lay in his damp bedroll "scribblin'" by firelight the final touches of his own message - *an ode to unrequited love.* He had worked on it feverishly since he and Master David rode out of New Washington. Henry titled it, *"Emily, Maid of Morgan's Point."*

> *"There's a yellow rose in Texas*
> *That I am going to see*
> *No other darky knows her,*
> *No one, only me.*
>
> *She cryed so when I left her*
> *It like to broke my heart*
> *And if I ever find her*
> *We nevermore will part.*
>
> *She's the sweetest rose of color*
> *This darky ever knew*
> *Her eyes are bright as diamonds*
> *They sparkle like the dew.*
>
> *You may talk about your dearest May*
> *Or sing of Rosa Lee*
> *But the yellow rose of Texas*
> *Beats the belles of Tennessee.*
>
> *~ HBC"*

Young Crockett's sentiments would later anonymously echo the spirit of the time and inspire countless generations - as much a part of history as Travis's urgent request for reinforcements.

Captain Albert Martin and some 30 additional troops arrived at the Alamo on 1st March. On 3rd March Travis penned another emotional appeal:

"A blood-red banner flies from the Church of Bejar (sic), and in the camp above us, in token that the war is one of vengeance against the rebels. They have declared us as such. And demanded that we should surrender or be, one and all, put to the sword. Their threats have had no influence on me or my men, but to make all fight with desperation, and that high-souled courage which characterizes the patriot who is willing to die in defence of his country's liberty and his own honour."

The nearest significant reinforcements - about 400 men under command of Colonel James Fannin, were halted near Goliad with strict orders not to engage the enemy besieging the Alamo. Finally on 6th March, after enduring thirteen days of endless artillery barrages and repulsing three suicide charges by Mexican infantry dragoons and horse-mounted lancers, the Alamo fell to Santa Anna's forces. Throughout that afternoon and into the evening townspeople in San Antonio heard musket volleys at regular intervals inside the mission walls.

The following morning more than 180 corpses, including those of Jim Bowie, William Travis and David Crockett, were stacked unceremoniously near the Alamo gates. All had been shot from the front - either in the chest or head. It was later said that Crockett had been executed with his own long rifle - at his request, "tuh make shore th' damn Dragoons don't mess me up with a porely made piece." Some of the dead had been blindfolded, perhaps at their own request. Travis, it was later learned, had died on the wall in the initial assault.

Others - those earlier wounded, had been seated and tied to their chairs before being executed. No personal effects were missing. This time none had been mutilated or beheaded. The bizarre and brutal scene was punctuated by peaceful clumps of Bluebonnets - buffalo clover - just beginning to show their vibrant blue spring color in the morning sun near the mission gates.

Francisco Antonio Ruiz wrote in English in his diary on 8th March: " - *the gallantry of the few Texians who defended the Alamo was really wondered at by our army. Even the generals were astonished by their vigorous resistance and how dearly victory was bought by us. We burnt Texians, one-hundred and eighty-two. I was an eyewitness, for as Alcalde [mayor and city magistrate] of San Antonio, I was with some of the neighbours, collecting the dead bodies and placing them on the funeral pyre."*

As residents and city officials tried to bring some sort of order and dignity to this chaotic scene, they began to collect and organize personal effects of the dead - both those of the Alamo defenders and those of the more than 1600 Mexican troops who perished in the fight. One seemingly insignificant paper retrieved by Señor Ruiz from the body of a young black man was titled, *"Emily, Maid of Morgan's Point."* It appeared to be *a love poem or ode of some kind.* The dead man had no other papers, and Ruiz kept the document.

~

Emily West had little time to develop and implement detailed logistics plans to supply the Texas militia in the field or the volunteers from Tennessee, Kentucky, Georgia and elsewhere - now camped along the San Jacinto River and Buffalo Bayou. On 2nd March, Texas had defiantly declared its independence from Mexico. Barely a week later word reached New Washington that, after 13 days of holding their position against overwhelming odds, the Texas forces had been defeated as Santa Anna's army had stormed the Alamo, and all defenders had been summarily executed. The worst fears of those in New Washington had come true. On 16th March, David Burnet and Lorenzo de Zavala y Saenz were named interim president and vice president, respectively, of the new Republic of Texas. Burnet was an open critic of Sam Houston - de Zavala on the other hand, was confident of Houston's ability to rally the fragmented Texas army and turn it into a disciplined fighting force.

"You are my good friend, Excellency." James Morgan addressed the new vice president, and both men, eye to eye, sighed heavily. "Texas independence has been a long time coming and at considerable human cost already. These are dark times - our destiny is at hand, yet I fear we may not prevail. Even so I know that an American Texas is that matter you feel most strongly about in life. To be chosen vice-president is now unquestionably the proper course. I only wish you had a more favorable environment in which to savor the appointment."

"Captain Morgan, I am quite honored," de Zavala responded. "And," he smiled openly, "I would invite you to my office for a proper celebratory toast, except that it is perhaps too soon - and in any event - my office is now in transit. Even as we speak I leave New Washington to assist President Burnet in establishing the Capitol at Harrisburg." De Zavala continued, "and you, my friend, will soon be doing more than attending to the supply and support of our armies. General Sam Houston needs your military background and experience - now! I have set up a meeting between the two of you for tomorrow afternoon at his field headquarters in the town hall."

~

In the general's cramped and musty office, Sam Houston sat with rolled-up shirtsleeves, sipping occasionally from a small, corked medicine bottle. A broad-brimmed white straw hat lay next to him on the cluttered desk. The weather had finally broken. It was sunny and warmer than it had been since the previous October. Houston had his one window open to the noise and dust of troops drilling in the town square nearby. He spoke gruffly but with respect to the uniformed man standing at rigid attention in front of him. "Colonel Morgan, thank you for meeting with me on such short notice."

"General Houston, it is a privilege to meet you. How may Captain James Morgan, *(Continental Army-Retired)*, be of assistance to you, sir?" Morgan maintained a position of rigid attention, dressed in his old but well-pressed uniform. West and the hotel staff had made certain that Morgan was presentable for his meeting with General Houston. They needn't have bothered. Houston was not much for military formality. *He wanted results!*

No salutes were exchanged, and neither man had yet shaken hands. Seeing Houston's flask, Morgan thought *my God the general is a Laudanum addict. He had lost more than one acquaintance to this supposedly medicinal, powerfully addictive opiate he now suspected Houston was sipping.*

"Be at ease, Colonel Morgan and rest your bones. And for God's own sake and yours, unbutton that damned waistcoat and take a seat!" Houston gestured to a rough wooden chair that Morgan moved to.

With Morgan seated and now seemingly more relaxed in his unbuttoned jacket, Houston took another sip from the flask and continued. "Your orders as you will see, note your appointment as full colonel in the Army of the Texas Republic. This was at the Vice President's direction - not subject to dispute by either of us. My congratulations and Godspeed!" After a slight pause Houston abruptly stood and approached Morgan, extending his right hand that held a small sheaf of papers. Morgan stood as he accepted the promotion orders without comment and shook the General's hand.

Houston continued as he returned to his desk chair, "The Alamo has fallen to Santa Anna. My view? We should not have been engaged there in the first place!" Taking another sip from the flask, Houston went on. "An unfortunate loss of many loyal souls, including a great soldier, Colonel Bowie, and my fellow Tennessean and former Congressman, Colonel Crockett. But we can only be wiser, more cautious, from this defeat and from perhaps another in the making. I have just learned that Urrea has captured Fannin and his men at Goliad. It is my understanding that our troops surrendered peaceably and are being treated humanely by the Mexicans. I'm told they have been assured of their ultimate release. This is welcome news, but unfortunately I suspect it is not my friend Santa Anna's final order in this case. Whatever the outcome at Goliad, it's another defeat in the west and emphasizes that Mexican forces continue to bear down on us here in east Texas - with the intent that we shall never be independent.

"My staff and I must now devote our undivided efforts to countering this latest thrust from the cursed Mexicans, lest they run us into the Bay and Gulf of Mexico and we perish. As part of our plan, we must regroup and increase our numbers and fighting capability. To buy time for this to be realized, we must also have a strong and secure rear echelon - a final sanctuary, if you will. I am therefore ordering you, subject only to your conscience, to command the forces that will maintain the security of Galveston Island - reporting directly to me. This spit of land where the new seat of government may be required to reside is of great strategic importance to Texas and must not fall into Mexican hands. I expect you to determine what measures are appropriate to fortify the island against any eventual attack, and you will implement those measures without delay. Now - may I have the courtesy of your favorable reply within the hour?"

"Sir, I am not experienced in what you ask me to do," Morgan responded stiffly. "However with that said, my answer now is unquestionably - yes! Though I have business affairs that need to be addressed, I can be on the island within two days to assume my command, if that is acceptable. And I will work with your staff on the details."

"Thank you, Colonel Morgan. That is acceptable," responded Sam Houston as he rose to usher Morgan to the door.

Chapter Thirteen

"Emily," Morgan said, "I have issues that require our immediate attention! You know that the new Vice President of our republic, and our mutual friend, Señor de Zavala, will be required to be in the Texas capitol at Harrisburg or wherever it must move until we have defeated Santa Anna." West noted *no sarcasm in Morgan's description of her paramour.* "Yesterday afternoon I accepted an assignment from General Houston as Colonel in the Texas Army and commander of the forces on Galveston Island," he continued. "I am to see that the island is fortified sufficiently to repel any attack by Mexico, and I must be on the island in 48 hours. Thus, neither Señor de Zavala nor I will be available for direction or consultation on business affairs here until we are relieved of our responsibilities. Quite simply this means that the operation of the New Washington Hotel and Restaurant and the port I must now place in your hands. I am providing the necessary papers that authorize you to conduct business as you deem appropriate."

"I...I am near speechless, Captain...uh Colonel Morgan," West stammered. "I do not know at this moment how I will do what you ask, but I will do my best to conduct the businesses in a way that I feel you would approve. My highest priority will be to maintain the supplies in our fight with Mexico."

"That is all that I can ask, Emily," Morgan responded. "And please listen carefully because this is an order! If, at any time, you feel that you cannot safely conduct business in the restaurant, hotel, or on the docks, you are to immediately evacuate the premises and board the coastal steamer to Galveston Island. Do not let yourself be put in harm's way. Also, do not concern yourself with my house - and be ever vigilant because Mexican battle tactics include flying columns as advance parties or reconnaissance for their major troop movements. These forces are usually their elite men, and they can be lethal."

"I will be very careful, sir, I promise…" West's voice trailed off as Morgan briefly embraced her then crossed the hotel lobby and headed for the door.

~

On 26th March Sam Houston was bitterly engaged in yet another confrontation with his staff and local politicians regarding his defensive strategy versus the growing demands for some quicker means of counter-attack by Texas forces to avenge the Alamo defeat.

The day before General Santa Anna had impatiently paced the floor of his field headquarters in San Antonio de Béxar. His aides scurried past him, packing for the push eastward. The general fumed at the apparent reluctance of General Urrea to carry out his order to execute the Goliad prisoners. *What was it about Colonel Fannin and his detachment that required they be shown any more mercy than Travis, Bowie and their rebels at The Alamo? If we blink - if we show any kindness, these peasants with guns and knives will think us weak.* Santa Anna's new order to General Urrea was more specific and carried the unmistakable threat to his field commander that failure to finish the Goliad mission would be considered treason.

It was Palm Sunday, 27th March, when the roughly 300 uninjured troops of Colonel Fannin's command at Goliad were marched, in three separate columns, onto Béxar Road, San Patricio Road and Victoria Road. They were positioned opposite the ranks of Mexican riflemen, and Colonel Fannin was forced to watch as the crack and echo of rifle fire punctuated the annihilation of his detachment, one by one. After the roadside executions, Mexican troops clubbed or stabbed to death any Texans they could find who looked to be still alive, while other execution squads did their work on the 100 or so wounded Texians remaining in the nearby church courtyard.

Fannin was then personally escorted by General Urrea back into the same courtyard, put in a chair and blindfolded. His last requests, delivered verbally to the general, were to have his belongings sent to his family, to be shot in the chest - not the face or head, and to be given a Christian burial. Fannin was shot twice, point-blank in the face, and his body, along with all of his gear, was tossed onto the pile of other bodies and burned.

But despite this seemingly bloody, total massacre, more than 30 Texans survived - by playing dead. Some later spoke and wrote of the incident. News of the Goliad *"massacre"* closely following the Alamo siege became a "line in the sand" that Santa Anna had crossed - the tipping point that stiffened the resolve of new Texas. Their rallying cry became, *"Remember the Alamo - remember Goliad!"*

~

Less than two weeks later, many of the Texans and all of their new government officials were forced to flee the advancing Mexican Army once again, this time to Galveston Island, as Houston had earlier thought might be necessary. Before he left New Washington, de Zavala met with West at the hotel. "Emily, my wife and the children will be in danger at home very soon, particularly because of my prominent role in the republic. Thus far she has refused to come with me, and I relented. But we must send a boat to Zavala's Point and move them here to the hotel as soon as possible."

De Zavala now embraced West, drawing her close to him as he spoke further. "Should New Washington be threatened, and I fear it soon will, you must then move all of yourselves to Galveston Island. There can be no heroics. Leave this war to the men who started it. If all else fails and we men are lost, at least I know Generale Santa Anna to be one who treats non-combatants, particularly women and children, with respect."

"I will, my love - my Lorenzo. I will do as you are requesting," West responded. "But despite your assurances as to the Generale's mercy, he showed none of it, I am told, in the Zacatecas rebellion last year. Did he not take more than 3,000 souls prisoner and then give his army of operations two days to loot and rape the province as they wished?" De Zavala paled but said nothing, bestowing on West a final, gentle kiss. *That perfume is intoxicating. Wherever could she continue to find French perfume in Texas? But moreover, how does she know so much about Santa Anna's past military campaigns? Is there nothing that does not concern her? Does she trust no one?*

Chapter Fourteen

April 1836

"I do not want to leave my home. We are not in danger," Emilia de Zavala complained to the man at her side – as she quickly shepherded her three children up the gangplank to the small steam-powered workboat.

"Madam, you are in danger," the pilot sternly spoke. "Mexican troops approach ever closer. Your husband has instructed the port master to send my vessel to move you and your family at once to the hotel nearby."

"Captain! I see you are casting off, but I had a priceless chest of heirloom silver that I purchased in Paris. It is not aboard. Your men have either stolen it or failed to load it with the rest of our belongings. They must be sent to retrieve it without delay."

"Madam de Zavala, you speak of delay. There is, I regret, no time for such personal matters. We must depart immediately! I am sorry."

"Very well, captain," de Zavala said, "if we are in so much danger, then let us proceed directly to Galveston Island and dispense with this intermediate docking in the village."

"My instructions are to sail via the New Washington port. If Mexican forces are close, or it is otherwise unsafe for us to dock and retrieve Miss West and the remaining staff, she will fly a signal - a red ensign from the flag staff in the square."

"A pirate flag? Miss West would be so bold as to fly a buccaneer's signal? For what purpose may I enquire? This would seem to be quite mad," responded Emilia de Zavala.

"Madam, such a ruse would be used only in dire circumstances to warn us and to perhaps provide those ashore in New Washington some added time for escape. Most Mexicans, I dare say, are as concerned about these lawless men as we are. They would at least be required to stop momentarily, reassess their capability for combat and see to the true significance of the ensign." With that remark the pilot, having ordered the small boiler stoked, steered the craft away from the pier and into San Jacinto Bay.

~

Colonel Juan Almonte and his company of dragoons, dressed in their dark blue tunics with white cross-belts and matching white trousers, red feathered shakos atop mostly bearded heads - cast an awesome, threatening appearance crossing the fields. Their muskets were cradled at the ready, and sheathed bayonets slapped against their thighs, The elite Mexican troops moved quietly and steadily in a disciplined column through the scrub brush and sandy soil west of New Washington until they reached Zavala's Point. The hacienda was deserted, but smoldering kitchen fires told Almonte and his men that they had missed capturing the de Zavala family by no more than an hour. A large chest of silver still sat on the hallway floor - apparently forgotten in the family's haste to escape. From the expansive veranda a small harbor steamer was barely visible in the bay, moving south.

"Damn, we have missed capturing the traitor de Zavala's family by only a small window - so we are not yet successful!" Colonel Almonte swore and threw down his gloves as he spoke. "They will surely stop at New Washington, so leave two men with the chest of silver for our supply wagon. The rest of us will move on the New Washington settlement. We may overtake them or we may not, but the town will be burned to the ground and the port destroyed. This supply route must be neutralized."

~

Earlier that day, 16th April, hundreds of Tejano and Texian families on foot and horseback, their belongings on wagons or carts, passed the New Washington Hotel, headed northeast along the San Jacinto River to find fording points. Most of them had burned their modest barns and cabins before moving on - a scorched earth practice that Houston frowned upon and had futilely ordered to be stopped. West knew from hearing the fearful remarks of these refugees that the lead elements of Santa Anna's army were close. As she stood on the steps after lowering the new Texas Republic flag and running up a plain red ensign in the small town square, a bold but risky plan formed in West's mind.

~

Almonte and his dragoons were on the outskirts of New Washington village when one of the scouts reported back the absence of any citizenry and that there was no Mexican...or *Tejas* flag on the staff near town hall. "In her place", he informed Colonel Almonte, "is flying a plain red banner." The commander, pondering the meaning, suddenly broke out in raucous laughter. "Either we are surrounded by pirates - but Lafitte is long departed, and I see no ships at the moorings, or" - another hearty laugh - "whoever is left gives no quarter and will put us all to the sword if we do not surrender." His troops within hearing distance took up the laughter and it quickly spread through the nervous rank and file.

The moment of humor having passed, the colonel ordered the town torched. "Nothing will be left standing. If any residents are found, execute the men and bring any women and children into the town square to me. And", he admonished, "waste no ammunition!" Salutes and acknowledgements were exchanged, torches fired and the dragoons set about to begin their search and destroy mission.

Two dragoons entered the New Washington Hotel with torches. Moments later as Colonel Almonte looked on in disbelief, a hellish event took shape in the doorway. His corporal slowly exited the hotel shouldering the lifeless, bloody body of the dragoon who had accompanied him. A calm Emily West held a large knife to the corporal's neck with her left hand. Her right hand steadied the stock of one of the dragoon's muskets along her forearm. It was cocked and the muzzle was pointed approximately at Colonel Almonte. There was no smoke or fire coming from inside the hotel behind them.

West addressed the dragoon commander in recognizably proper Castillian Spanish, her cold green eyes flashing. "Colonel which meaning did you believe my red ensign to have? I trust not as a signal that there were pirates about?" Before the startled and chagrined Colonel could muster a response to what amounted to a beautiful but already deadly apparition, West continued. "You could end my life at any moment - but not without you and the corporal here accompanying me. And there has already been quite enough killing today." She gestured with her head toward the lifeless form on the corporal's shoulder. "Your poor private would agree if he but had life left to speak. I am not as I appear, nor is my manservant inside who stands now behind the window with your other musket. You may burn this village as you wish - take all the spoils you can find. We are not your enemy. I have only a single demand - safe passage at once for me and my attendant to Generale Lopez de Santa Anna - wherever he is quartered."

Colonel Almonte, his right arm raised as a signal for his nearby dragoons, standing at the ready, not to fire, spoke anxiously. "Excellency, Señora - Señorita? My God, whom do I address? Where do you come from - whom do you represent?"

"My name and our credentials are not for you to question, commander. I am aware of your Generale Lopez de Santa Anna's dislike for the Bourbons and their decimation of true Spain, and I know of his sentiments in the Carlist War now raging in Spain's heartland. Such a struggle is not unlike your own to keep this land we call Tejas for Mexico - and Spain." West made a sweeping gesture with the musket around the square, causing more than one dragoon to momentarily flinch. "I have information that can only be discussed with your commandante in person. Those are my orders - my demands. This intelligence will give him the means to finally subdue these rebellious Anglos and locals and restore the prominence of Mexico and Spain to North America. God does not wish us to sell out Tejas to these psuedo-patriot land mongers as France sold Louisiana to Jefferson. So either take us now or let us perish together. Your choice, I believe, is clear!"

With a cautious, sweeping bow, Colonel Almonte offered his right hand to West - his dragoons immediately easing their musket hammers into lock position and lowering their weapons. West too, leaned the uncocked musket to her side and permitted Almonte to put his pursed lips to her right hand. A relieved corporal pushed the bowie knife gingerly away from his neck, knelt and eased the corpse from his shoulders. He was sweating profusely. West maintained her regal faux Spanish arrogance as she summoned her manservant, Turner Metoyer, a young Creole man, who spoke passable Spanish and French, in addition to English. As he came off the hotel veranda and into the square, first Metoyer, then West handed over their weapons to Almonte.

Within the hour New Washington had been torched. After a small evening meal in what was left of the village square, the entourage set off toward the main Mexican army encampment, now less than two miles away. Almonte mused as he rode alongside West and her manservant *what a prize this one is! She is certainly my generale's taste - in looks, in spirit and in combat prowess. She will be like no one he has ever met. I may earn my star with this mission, even if the de Zavalas are temporarily still at large.*

~

The pilot had just begun his approach toward the New Washington docks when he saw the red ensign being raised in the town square. He quickly steered to port and steamed wide of New Washington toward Galveston Island. A faint smile played across Emilia de Zavala's face. *Madam West must be shocked and frightened indeed to see her last hope disappear.* By sunset the pilot brought his craft safely to anchor off the east end of Galveston Island. Dinghies brought the de Zavala family and their belongings to shore.

James Morgan and Lorenzo de Zavala listened as the ship's pilot recounted the story of the 30-mile passage from Zavala's Point, past New Washington and Morgan's Point, to Galveston Island. Morgan bit down hard on his unlit cigar as he was briefed. The pilot could not determine what had happened to West, but verified that a red ensign had been run up the flagstaff in the town center at about the time his lookout spotted a company-sized Mexican troop unit moving west-to-east on the outskirts of New Washington. The pilot reported hearing no shots fired. Morgan and de Zavala *were concerned, but furious that West had acted precisely against their orders. Even so they reckoned that Emily West, as strikingly attractive and resourceful as she was, had a better than even chance of survival in enemy hands. With the main Mexican force now probably not more than a few miles west of the San Jacinto River, they needed to get quickly to the business of fortifying Galveston Island as much as possible.*

Chapter Fifteen

It was nearing midnight on the 17th April when Colonel Juan Almonte led his company of Dragoons in their passage through the scattered lines of the main Mexican Army force now camped on the plains just southwest of Buffalo Bayou and the San Jacinto River. West and her freeman, Turner Metoyer, had ridden tandem for the short march across darkened fields, but they had been treated well and left unrestrained. Once in camp West and Metoyer we're searched again, given water and put in separate, guarded tents while Almonte reported to an awaiting and impatient General Lopez de Santa Anna.

Before Colonel Almonte could do much more than begin his after-action report, Santa Anna broke in. "So - I am correct? Yes? You tell me, Colonel Almonte, that you have failed to bring me the de Zavala family? All you managed was to sack the village and bring me a crate of kitchen silver and two prisoners - one a Negro slave - the other a Spaniard...or perhaps a Béxareno - a woman who bested two of your elite troops with nothing more than a common butcher's knife? Now you stand before me and insist I will be most pleased with your success? How can that be?" The Army Commander, chewing at a small wad of chicle in one cheek, appeared irritated and as fatigued as his troops, who had all now finally been ordered to stand down for at least 48 hours. Their siege of the Alamo, matters at Goliad and their forced march across much of east Texas in pursuit of the Texians had taken its toll. They had outrun much of their munitions and rations resupply, had exhausted infantry and horses, had few artillery pieces in camp and were short of fresh water. All but the General, his staff and those with operational surveillance missions or on guard duty, were now dressed in white camp fatigue uniforms.

Though battle-weary himself, Colonel Almonte enthusiastically used his chance to again address General Santa Anna. "Sir, my honorable Commander, as to the hostages you spoke about, I have brought with me one who appears to be one of Béxar's most beautiful flowers, an hidalgo (aristocrat) I am certain - with manservant - who demanded safe passage for a meeting with only you. She insists she has information that will materially aid us in subduing these rebellious fools, these Texians - for good! As you know I am not one who lightly agrees to such demands from prisoners of war. However when you meet this emissary, you will understand that she is indeed as she claims, representing loyal Mexicans of Spanish heritage and is a powerful ally. You will, I am confident, agree with my actions."

Barely five hours later Emily West was summoned from her tent and taken to General Santa Anna's sprawling, tented compound - presumably for a breakfast meeting. Inside the general's tent she saw there was only Turner Metoyer, smiling slightly and ready to serve morning coffee - along with General Lopez de Santa Anna himself. The general was pouring a clear liquid – (Laudanum?) from a small flask into his ornate china cup. Santa Anna was dark and slightly weathered from his years in the sun. His hair was cropped short and the general was clean-shaven. Santa Anna was dressed only in white trousers and dark silk morning shirt and wore slippers without stockings. He stood as West entered. *Santa Anna was more handsome, but shorter, than she had imagined. He smiled easily and openly but he was not easy to read* West thought.

General Santa Anna spoke. "Señorita Leonora Delgado, as your man Turner tells me you are known – you are presumably from one of the fine Béxareno families of San Antonio de Béxar, loyal to Mexico and Spain. To what do I owe the pleasure and considerable honor of your noble company? And moreover what might you have been doing yesterday in the poor Anglo hamlet of New Washington?"

"Excellency, we have made no such claims of nobility." West responded as she was offered a seat beside the general. "We present no credentials of diplomacy. Yet I and my aide are most grateful for your indulgence. We have waited and planned many months for this rendezvous."

West continued her deception by describing in detail, this time in flawless military jargon, how Santa Anna might finally overwhelm the Texian regulars and volunteers. She described launching the Mexican force's final attack along two fronts - the primary assault northeast toward the San Jacinto River against Houston's main force, and a smaller more elite detachment ferrying across the channel to Galveston to seize and destroy the new Texas government and its headquarters. She insisted that the main attack should be on or after 21st April, but not before.

As she went on to explain, this would be the earliest that Houston would be able to regroup and consolidate his entire militia west of the river. The Texas army would then be concentrated, but still in defensive positions and vulnerable to surprise assault. Although a fabrication *Santa Anna appeared to take the false intelligence seriously, considering other details West had given him about Houston's reluctance to commit relief forces to the earlier defense of the Alamo mission. Further,* West stated, in response to his concern about her presence in New Washington that *she had frequently been a guest at the New Washington Hotel on family business with local merchants. She had always used these visits to judge the Texians' capability and resolve.* It appeared to Santa Anna that the woman *was not in favor of a Texas Republic, nor was she any friend of Anglos.*

General Santa Anna's countenance brightened considerably as he thought about West's proposal. *He knew the timing she described was acceptable. By then he should have ample reinforcements and supplies. His army should be rested. Any time after the 21st he'd be ready. He would also give Colonel Almonte and his company of dragoons a chance to redeem themselves. They would be the Galveston strike force, the flying company.*

The general spoke. "Some have described me as

'Napoleon de Mexico.' But I am **not** Bonaparte. And Sam Houston I expect is no Wellington. And certainly this San Jacinto ground will not be 'Waterloo!' My command will act immediately to investigate your proposal. If they report back that the Texian rebels are moving to consolidate as you indicate, and we can then prevail over Houston and that damnable traitor, de Zavala, you will have Mexico's undying gratitude. If all is not as you say, then unfortunately - it is simply you and your man here who may die." Santa Anna looked first to Metoyer then back to West, fixing his dark, unblinking eyes on hers.

West did not take her eyes from Santa Anna's as she responded. "Excellency we would expect no less. Their troop movements will be as I have said - but I cannot guarantee you will prevail. Only God in his mercy may do that! I can though suggest that your reconnaissance force take my attendant with them" - nodding toward Metoyer - "he has spent more time in this eastern Texas territory than you or I, and certainly he has no love of his former masters. He can aid your people considerably in their probing action." Touching the general's arm, she continued, "Meanwhile I look forward to your continued hospitality here in your very comfortable compound." West's almost open flirtation with Santa Anna at this point was enough to cause him to ponder silently *what social and sexual pleasures he might enjoy while most of his army got some much needed respite from battle. He had been away from his new wife in Mexico for months now. So despite strong objections from some of his staff later that they were too vulnerable, camped in the open plains less than two miles from a growing enemy threat, Santa Anna stood down.*

Neither General Santa Anna nor his latest consort was much in evidence in camp all day the 18th and well into the next day. To the dismay of his general staff, the Mexican Army of more 700 continued to languish, camped in the open plain, protected only by a rudimentary stockade of saplings, saddles and saddlebags, constructed hastily between them and the Texian force. Although vulnerable, they knew that *reinforcements were near.* On 20th April General Cos arrived as planned from the west with another 500 men, giving Santa Anna numerical superiority. Cos's troops after their long march, pitched tents, unrolled bedding, donned their white camp uniforms and became part of a now greatly enlarged, although less organized bivouac.

Late in the evening of the 20th and little over a mile and a half to the northeast - barely three hundred yards from the forward elements of Houston's army, freeman Turner Metoyer, crawled silently away from the exhausted, sleeping reconnaissance squad he had accompanied. West had given him his strict instructions. "Wait for darkness, and when they sleep, somehow be off. You MUST escape and make your way to the Texians. Surrender to them by waving a white kerchief, tied firmly to a long stick, three times. When they see that you are colored and hear that you are not Mexican, they will not harm you. Make them take you immediately to General Houston where you will give him the location, disposition, strength and condition of the Mexicans."

West had continued Metoyer's orders. "Tell him he must first destroy Vince's Bridge to prevent any escape - and he must attack no later than the afternoon siesta on the day after tomorrow, the 21st. Soon after that the Mexican reinforcements of general Cos will have been rested and be ready for combat. And any time after that day Santa Anna may also have received more artillery pieces." Turner did precisely as he was ordered. Houston and his staff indeed listened attentively.

~

It was nearing the hour of the siesta, early afternoon on 21st April, and in the general's compound, Santa Anna was immensely enjoying his respite from combat. *He had never been with anyone as worldly, as beautiful, nor as sexually aggressive and combative as this woman. Was she a Béxareno - or Spanish, French, Creole - did it matter? Obviously she could defend herself in almost any situation. A bowie knife and her small, ivory handled Chatellerault, had been retrieved by Santa Anna from Colonel Almonte and, at the General's insistence, secured in his bedroom field chest.* "Leonora Delgado - whoever you are - wherever you come from, God in his mercy sent you to me. I have been in too many battles, too long away from the comfort of a woman's body and moreover, have had little intellectual or social stimulation from these jackals I call my staff!" Santa Anna lay naked on his bed with West propped up beside him, partly covered in a bed sheet. She smiled as she spoke. "My dear Lopez de Santa Anna, wars make enemies of friends and lovers of strangers. We should not question why fate put us together. Rather let us continue to enjoy our moment's passion. Is it not sufficient that your Colonel Almonte found me and brought me to you?" General Santa Anna could only nod his agreement as he buried his head against her bosom, and she stroked his bare neck and shoulders.

Later, their passion abated, the two now sat on a couch in the general's tented quarters and drank glasses of Misión Blanco while they had lunch. Santa Anna had fortified his wine with his ever-present flask of Laudanum. They were both dressed in proper day attire now in case the general was required to meet with his staff - the general in a dark navy tunic and white waistcoat, both unbuttoned to reveal a crisp white shirt. Santa Anna had pulled on his black riding boots. West had been provided an elegant pale orange and yellow striped linen skirt and yellow blouse from the general's wardrobe trunk. Her boots had been properly cleaned and shined by one of Santa Anna's orderlies. She wondered silently *how many other women might have worn this same attire…and where they were.*

At the entrance to the general's tent a lone sentry, a private of the President's Own Dragoons, stood watch. West spoke first. "My dearest lover, my emperor, you are indeed the great hope of all the people of Tejas, of Mexico - perhaps of the whole Americas." She paused for emphasis before continuing. "But I fear your Catholic upbringing has deprived you of many of the passions of love and life. In bed surprisingly you are not the great emperor, the President of Mexico nor are you the genius of the battlefield. No, regrettably the general is a mere Catholic schoolboy, a commoner who chews rubber and enjoys only the boring sexual position favored by the Jesuit and Franciscan missionaries."

The general put his glass down, and his dark eyes narrowed as West went on. "You should broaden your appetites and improve your manners - and I shall help you in these endeavors, once we have put these rebels to the sword!" *West was not averse to intercourse with Santa Anna - in fact she enjoyed it to a degree. But she disliked the rubbery, medicinal smell of the chicle the general often chewed - the latex-like product of the chicle bush, and a daily indulgence of most Mexican peasants. Most of all, though, she wanted the general thinking of her and nothing else for the next few hours.*

Lopez de Santa Anna reddened and moved away on the couch. *He had never had such* **criticisms** *- no, such* **insults** *- of any kind, anywhere, hurled at him - by anyone! This arrogant woman dares to question my religion, my manners, my ability to love, my very manhood - the essences of my being? I am supposed to make* **her** *happy?* He fumed, sputtered and then silently collected himself. Finally Santa Anna addressed West quietly. "Señorita Delgado, you are perhaps the most beautiful, charming and intelligent woman I have ever known. Your presence, your appearance, even your aroma - they enchant me. You appear as a bouquet of roses in summer. But pondering now these many rude remarks, I am certain that you are truly no hidalgo -more likely just a commoner - someone's prickly thorn of Béxar!" West maintained her emotionless pleasant demeanor despite the general's retorts. Santa Anna concluded, "I have no idea what I shall do with you" – he sighed mightily as he reached for her hand – "but I think I cannot live without you."

~

General Sam Houston had finished his "war council" early in the morning on the 21st, taking into consideration all that he and his staff had learned from Turner Metoyer. There was a consensus of sorts - the enemy though recently reinforced was weakened and somewhat disorganized. Santa Anna's forces were still short of supplies, exhausted from long marches and had built only improvised battlements on the open plain - and they were pinned on the east and north sides by the recently flooded Buffalo and Vince's Bayous, and by Galveston Bay to the south. They had dragoons and lancers, but were short of artillery. For the last three days Santa Anna had ordered "all possible rest in evenings and during siesta" - posting only the most essential sentries inside the camp and employing no forward scouts or skirmishers facing the Texian army positions to their east, other than the one reconnaissance squad still out - the hapless one that freeman Turner Metoyer had escaped from. Sam Houston hoped - correctly as it turned out - *that this unit had not made it back to report their failure.*

Although some, including Houston himself were still concerned that *the army was not ready for decisive battle*, by one o'clock that afternoon, a battle plan had been developed, and the Texian Army was moving into positions for the surprise attack. The sun was out, and the plains were drying. Spring had turned the fields around the encampment blue with buffalo clover, but the marshes near the bayous on the Mexican flank were still almost impassable masses of mud. By mid-afternoon Houston received the first piece of good news from one of the mounted scouts. The bridge over Vince's Bayou had indeed been burned by "Deaf" Smith and his sappers without them being detected.

Most of the more than 600 Texian infantrymen, volunteers and regulars, were shielded from the Mexican camp by a grove of trees to the south and a low ridge line stretching across the open plain. In hindsight this ridge was where General Santa Anna should have insisted on a forward observation post or a line of skirmishers for early warning.

Mirabeau Lamar, a Georgia boy who loved a good fight and had engaged in more than one act of heroics for Houston, was promoted the day before from private to brevet colonel and placed in command of the cavalry unit of some 60 well-armed riders. The three regimental infantry units in the center were supported by two brass, smooth-bore cannons and ammunition donated to the cause earlier by sympathetic citizens of Cincinnati, Ohio. Cincinnatians had learned of the New Washington Association and its support of Texas liberty from Frenchmen Alexis de Tocqueville and Gustave de Beaumont. They wanted to help.

The "Twin Sisters" as they were affectionately known, were supplied with ample stacks of deadly grapeshot, and their gunners now knew where to lay down withering fire in support of what would be a frontal assault by infantry, coordinated with a flanking cavalry charge. Captain Isaac Moreland commanded the artillery. Houston himself commanded the infantry, but from horseback, saying, "I am too goddam slow of foot to walk to war."

Shortly after three o'clock at Houston's signal, the infantry began its silent advance. As they crested the ridge there were two regiments on line, one accompanied by Houston on horseback, and a third regiment in reserve. A lone fifer began to play, *"Will you come to the bower I have shaded for you,"* a favorite song of Sam Houston and the signal to ready the first infantry volley. Mexican troops, some just exiting their tents and some sitting in the mid-afternoon sun, first heard the fife music then saw the line of infantry moving toward them some 200 yards to their northeast. In that same instant the Texas infantrymen all but disappeared from Mexican view behind a solid line of grey-blue muzzle smoke. Less than a second later, both the weapons' thunder and over 400 musket balls from Houston's infantry volley arrived, cutting down most of the standing Mexicans at the edge of the encampment. Where there should have been order and resolve, panic set in. Mexican dragoons, themselves accustomed to firing volleys in disciplined ranks, now scattered haphazardly, most still in their white fatigues - some carrying weapons - some trying to don their combat gear. Cries of "They come! They come!!" echoed through the campsite.

Sam Houston signaled his troops to crouch, reload and prepare for a return volley from the enemy. The reserve regiment moved forward on line through the forward ranks for closer support and prepared to quickly fire a second volley. No organized return fire came from Santa Anna's troops. Instead only scattered rounds of musket fire whistled overhead or struck the ground in front of his lines. Two artillery rounds rattled the air and struck more than a hundred yards to the rear of where the third regiment had been in reserve.

Realizing he had completely surprised the Mexicans, Houston now raised a sword, wheeled his horse and rode hard toward the enemy - the signal for an all-out assault. Captain Moreland's "Twin Sisters" boomed their first salvos of grapeshot into the center of the bivouac, shredding white tents and white fatigues indiscriminately. In less than three minutes the two cannons had bloodied half the camp center, left more than a hundred scattered Mexican bodies and wounded many more. Charging Texian infantry screamed what would much later be known as "rebel yells" and took up the rallying cry - *"Remember the Alamo - remember Goliad!"* Retribution was at hand.

By the time the Texas infantry had made their way well into the northeastern part of the camp, sometimes fighting fiercely hand-to-hand, Mexican Colonel Juan Almonte had at least been able to assemble his company of dragoons into a battle formation. For moments they fought valiantly - standing their ground until Lamar's cavalry, charging in from one flank, hacked and trampled most of the elite Mexican unit into bloody tunics and mangled torsos where they stood. Colonel Almonte somehow survived the onslaught, unscathed.

Barely ten minutes into Houston's attack, the Mexicans

sounded a general retreat, sending their remaining infantrymen and lancers, those who had been able to assemble, toward the bridge at Vince's Bayou. Most of these unfortunate souls, finding the charred bridge in ruins, tried to ford or swim the 10-foot deep water. Many drowned. Those who did not were either shot in the water by Texian infantry from the bayou bank or slaughtered as they slipped and staggered up the muddy slopes.

~

In the general's compound, positioned well to the west side of the campsite, Lopez de Santa Anna and Emily West heard the first sounds of the attack from the east. To West's surprise the general made no move to retrieve his personal weapons or his uniform. Instead Santa Anna calmly ordered his sentry into the tent vestibule, directed him to strip to his underwear and sent West to the sleeping quarters. As she silently observed through the loose door flap, the general in charge of all the armies of Mexico, and its self-styled president, transformed himself into a lowly private of the dragoons. Santa Anna, now in uniform but weaponless, exited the compound through the front tent flaps without farewell.

Minutes later West pried open the lock, retrieved her knives from Santa Anna's field chest and crawled out under the canvas tent wall. As she made her way toward the perimeter, West encountered two dragoons viciously clubbing and hacking at a wounded Texian cavalryman. His saddle cinch had apparently broken, spilling him to the ground, and his mount was gone. She dispatched one dragoon with a deadly, flat trajectory toss of her bowie knife - an upper rib cage strike to his back that punctured one lung and severed his aorta. He was dead before his body, face first, hit dirt. The second Mexican surrendered to West without fanfare as she held the smaller switchblade in one hand and knelt over the corpse, struggling without success to extract the massive blade, buried to its hilt.

Colonel Mirabeau Lamar saw the encounter from horseback as he was racing through mangled tents, dead, dazed and wounded combatants and battlefield debris. He drew up quickly - summoning two of his mounted troopers to take the startled Mexican into custody. Reaching down to West, he hoisted the woman he'd met last at the New Washington Hotel onto his horse behind him. Emily West was delivered to the vicinity of Captain Isaac Moreland and his crews manning the "Twin Sisters" as Lamar returned to his "mop-up" chores. She was grimy and sweating through her borrowed yellow blouse - grateful to be back among "friendlies." But West harbored two lingering thoughts: *the whereabouts of "dragoon private" Lopez de Santa Anna - and, with Bowie killed at the Alamo, how she might obtain another broad knife.*

The Battle of San Jacinto had lasted less than twenty minutes. More than 700 Mexicans had died, and over 300 more were wounded, adding to an equal number of prisoners. Very few had escaped to make it back to Mexico and tell their story. Houston's troops meanwhile had suffered only seven dead and twenty wounded, although the reluctant Texas Army commander himself had lost two horses shot from under him and nearly lost an ankle to a musket ball. Sam Houston now sat quietly on his horse blanket under a spreading live oak tree and sipped Laudanum - for the pain.

Chapter Sixteen

The late afternoon Texas sun cast long shadows across the blanket Sam Houston still occupied. He had been having his wound attended and was receiving after-action reports from field commanders. In the distance a lone, bareheaded Mexican dragoon, accompanied by three heavily armed Texas militiamen, slowly approached the live oak where the general nursed his small, half empty flask. Houston immediately recognized James Sylvester, Second Sergeant and flag bearer of his First Texas Volunteer Regiment, leading the closely guarded Mexican. Those observing the four men as they reached Houston saw the Mexican introduce himself to the seated general, shake Houston's proffered right hand and be offered a place opposite him on the blanket. It was General Lopez de Santa Anna. Conspiracy theorists later alleged that the Mexican general had given Sam Houston, a Masonic brother, the sign of distress of the Freemasons - the "secret handshake" - as they met, thus earning him a reprieve from immediate execution.

The Mexican general spoke in halting English, with occasional translation from one of the Texians guarding him. "It was my wish to meet you personally, General Houston, and to convey my sincerest apologies for this most difficult circumstance. Many of our finest young men have, they have - died or been wounded in the, the" - Santa Anna's speech was now slurred - "struggles between our peoples. Now I believe - the time for hostilities may be over - if...if - you will accept my unconditional promise that my army lays down its arms." In that moment Sam Houston accepted the informal surrender of the Mexican Army - some said - *simply in exchange for a spare flask of Houston's Laudanum to calm the enemy general's frayed nerves.*

For his part that afternoon Houston made no extensive demands other than a requirement that Mexico formally recognize the legitimate independence of the new Republic of Texas, concluding that, "In exchange I shall work to the best of my ability and influence to see that you, General Santa Anna, are treated honorably. I will see that you return to Mexico as soon as practical with the freedom to pursue your remaining years in peace and prosperity."

But Houston was not able to keep his promise entirely. The following month Lopez de Santa Anna and Texas Republic Interim President, David G. Burnet signed the Treaties of Velasquez. In them Mexico was pledged by Lopez de Santa Anna to recognize the "full, entire and perfect independence of the Republic of Texas." But in Mexico City the new government refused to recognize the general's authority to sign any treaty or to accept Santa Anna's return to Mexico. For another few months Santa Anna would remain in captivity, and it would be another decade with another war against its southern neighbor before Texas could truly call itself free of Mexico.

Meanwhile many Texians were furious with interim president Burnet, de Zavala, the vice president, and Sam Houston for not executing General Santa Anna. Burnet bore the brunt of most of these accusations - resigning as interim president soon after the San Jacinto victory. US President Andrew Jackson though, had been the most powerful influence for saving the Mexican general - strongly urging both Sam Houston and the Texas president to spare Santa Anna. Jackson repeatedly made his point that Santa Anna was worth more to the US and the new Texas Republic as a live hostage - a powerful deterrent - than a dead martyr.

~

Emily West, the silent heroine and a combat veteran of the Texian victory over Santa Anna's army, now had a personal problem. *She was without housing or a job and, although she was a freeperson, she was one without any proper documents.* All her employment papers from James Morgan, as well as her travel authorizations, had perished when Almonte and his dragoons torched New Washington. Even so West was not without resources or aid. When confronted with official demands for identity and status shortly after independence broke out in east Texas, she turned to Captain Isaac Moreland for assistance, reasoning that *Captain Moreland after all was the officer who had provided her with refuge on the battlefield as he commanded the "Twin Sisters" cannon battery. And he had seen and heard as much as anyone else about her circumstances in Santa Anna's camp.*

"Thank you for speaking up for me, Captain Moreland," a grateful Emily West said. "I did not realize just how fragile my situation was without documents. And with Colonel Morgan and Vice President de Zavala unreachable at the moment, I had no one to vouch for me. You know my status and what happened on the battlefield, but there are few who would believe me. So at least until I can find Captain – rather, Colonel Morgan, may I consider myself at your disposal?"

"Madam, you need offer me neither thanks nor explanation. I could judge from your reported actions by Colonel Lamar - combat against armed men at considerable odds - that you are indeed a Tejano patriot. Further General Houston and his staff most certainly are aware that you dispatched your associate, the young man Metoyer, from Santa Anna's camp with valuable intelligence. That said, General Houston will certainly expect me to remain on active duty at least until the treaties are signed, and I suspect that he will want Colonel Morgan to do the same."

With West raptly attentive, Moreland continued. "Surely Colonel Morgan will want to rebuild the hotel and restaurant as soon as he is relieved of duty, but that will take some months, at least. My property has not been damaged by the Mexicans, and my family can use your assistance for several weeks if you choose to so accept. You need lodging, food and time to recover from your ordeal. May we plan for you to be with us until we have a chance to talk to Colonel Morgan?"

"Captain Moreland," West responded with a slight bow of her head and grasp of Moreland's outstretched hand, "How may I express my gratitude to you and Mrs. Moreland for this offer. I most graciously accept your hospitality and will take my direction from Mrs. Moreland as to what needs attending in your household."

Thank you, Lord, West was relieved in her musings two days after arriving at the Morelands. *My monthly time - and just on time! I most certainly did not want the burden of carrying a child of Santa Anna's. Mama Hemings always warned us girls at Monticello we should only have sex eight days before and eight days after our female time. Otherwise, we'd get pregnant. Of course, a fine example Mama Hemings set,* she smiled to herself - *six children with Mr. Jefferson. Oh well - don't do as I do, do as I say I do.*

~

"Lorenzo, my husband," Emilia de Zavala called out, "we have been on this, this - Galveston Island now for two months. When will we be able to return to Zavala's Point? I am not complaining about our accommodations - they are most adequate. But I did not realize how much I could miss old surroundings. When will the army finally be moving out of our house?" The de Zavala property had escaped burning by Colonel Almonte's unit, but because Lorenzo de Zavala and the rest of the new Texas government continued to operate out of Galveston, de Zavala had loaned his house to the army as a temporary surgical and rehabilitation facility. Emilia went on, "and I am curious too about Colonel Morgan's hotel manager and housekeeper, Emily West. You have heard the gossip - she met General Santa Anna during her capture. Some say she may even have gotten word to General Houston that helped him surprise the Mexican Army? I know she is at this moment working in the Moreland household, and they vouch for her character as well as her valor against the Mexicans.

"Perhaps I misjudged Miss West earlier. I confess that I harbored thoughts that she was more than a business associate of yours. We can say I was jealous, maybe envious of your time together? But we should put that behind us. And if she requires more stable employment, should we not hire her for Zavala's Point - particularly while your duties require so much family absence?"

De Zavala, *his mild surprise and exasperation evident,* replied. "The Army I'm told is already off our property, but it will be several weeks before it's in a state of proper sanitation. You and the children can perhaps return by the end of May. I on the other hand must remain in my present capacity here on the island for some months. As for Emily West, she was captured, but survived without being harmed. She is, as you say, working for Mrs. Moreland and staying in their servant's quarters while Captain Moreland remains on active duty. The stories about her may be true - but more probably people are simply looking for heroes. Miss West is certainly resourceful and capable of her own defense. As for my fondness for her, I admit only to the attraction any man has for beauty, for courage, for business acumen - particularly in a woman of her station. Beyond that - there is nothing between us." - *and someday I may, God willing, be able to forget that rainy afternoon in New Orleans,* de Zavala thought.

De Zavala continued, "Colonel Morgan and I have discussed rebuilding the hotel and restaurant. If that were practical now, with the growth we expect in this new republic, there would be employment for Emily West and ten more like her. But it is of little moment at the present, because General Houston has asked that Colonel Morgan remain on active duty until at least the end of the year. I will approach Captain Moreland and Colonel Morgan with the thought that we would be happy to employ Miss West more permanently if they have no immediate need for her services."

Chapter Seventeen

The late September sun was still warm, even though darkness came sooner and brought welcome relief from the heat and humidity of the Texas summer of 1836. It had been wetter than usual, and harvests were abundant. Livestock were fat and ready for slaughter. Emily West and Turner Metoyer were working near the limestone storage shed on the de Zavala property near the banks of San Jacinto Bay. The wagonload of provisions, grain and potatoes and fresh meat for the smokehouse was almost unloaded. Without warning they heard Emilia de Zavala's shriek as she called frantically to the two from the rear porch of the house. "Come quick, hurry! Hurry! Turner, you must fetch Doctor Emerson straightaway. Tell him it is Lorenzo and Augustine! He must help! Now! GO!"

Metoyer, who had been West's assistant at the New Washington Hotel and her accomplice in the San Jacinto battle, ran hard for the village center and Doctor Jonathan Emerson's office. West rushed in and followed Emilia de Zavala into the foyer. She found both Lorenzo de Zavala and his son Augustine lying on the floor, completely soaked and barely breathing - exhausted from what had been a routine canoe outing on San Jacinto Bay that had gone terribly wrong. The boat had apparently capsized. Unable to properly right it, the father had pulled his son onto its midsection then swam to shore, pushing the overturned canoe in the chilly waters as he went.

Augustine recovered within days. But Lorenzo de Zavala - weakened by a life of harassment and jail in Mexico, exile in New York, perhaps too much of the good life in Paris and the stress of leadership in the New Washington

Association and the new Republic - succumbed to pneumonia within weeks.

On 5th November 1836, Lorenzo de Zavala, laboriously, and without verbalizing a farewell to family or friends, breathed his last. Two grief-stricken women, each of whom he had known intimately, wrapped their arms about each other and cried unashamedly. *How could this man - leader, lover, father, and hero - be dead at only 47 years? His future was too bright for this to happen.* How indeed! All Texas mourned his loss. The flag of the new republic, the word *"Texas"* surrounding a lone white star on a field of blue, designed by de Zavala himself, flew at half-staff everywhere. Its congress passed resolutions of regret and adjourned in respect for their late vice president. Both the Telegraph and Texas Register of 26th November posted his obituary:

"Died on the 5th inst. at his residence on the San Jacinto, our distinguished and talented fellow citizen, Lorenzo De Zavala. In the death of this enlightened and patriotic statesman, Texas has lost one of her most valuable citizens - the cause of liberal principles, one of its most untiring advocates and society, one of its brightest ornaments. His travels have procured him an extensive acquaintance with mankind - his writings have justly elevated him to a high rank as an author - and the part he has played in the revolution of his country and his uncompromising exertions in favor of Republican institutions have erected to his memory a monument more durable than brass. His death will be lamented by the admirable and interesting family which he has left and the large number of friends which he has acquired through a life devoted to the cause of liberty and the service of mankind."

James Morgan, nearly speechless with grief, had laid his cigar stub aside and penned his thoughts, "My friend, comrade in peace and war, will be remembered as a man of integrity. Texas has lost its most ardent patriot." Santa Anna in captivity, when asked about de Zavala's ties to Mexico, was said to have commented only that, "he was always a part of Mexico's conscience." In his eulogy, one legislative colleague noted that, following the defeat of Santa Anna's army at San Jacinto, de Zavala offered his nearby home as a hospital for both Texan and Mexican wounded soldiers. Another colleague's eulogy spoke of his intense desire for Texas to be independent by quoting de Zavala's most inspiring statement:

"If I knew my death would assure the liberation of Texas, I would not live another hour."

~

Captain Isaac Moreland walked the short hallway to the Texas state secretary's office for his morning appointment. He had directed Emily West to sit on a bench against the corridor wall, in case her services were needed. She waited nervously as her sponsor went in to his meeting with Doctor Robert A. Irion, Secretary of State of the Texas Republic. Moreland, addressing the Secretary began, "Your Honor, may I say first 'thank you' for serving the Republic of Texas and for making this time to see me. With your permission, I shall get straight to the point. I am here to request a passport for my client and former employee, Emily D. West. She is a woman of color who has given her best in the defense of our new republic and deserves recognition as of one of our own. Trusting that you are authorized to act upon my request, I have prepared this letter" - handing the paper over to the secretary who read the handwritten document:

"Capitol, Thursday morning
To the Hon. Dr. Irion
The bearer of this-Emily d. West has been since my first

acquaintance, in April of –36 a free woman---she Emigrated to this
Country with Col. Ja's Morgan from the State of N. York in
September of 35 and is now anxious to return and wishes a passport-
---I believe myself, that she is entitled to one and has requested me to
give this note to you.

Your Obd Serv't
I.N. Moreland
Her free papers were Lost at San Jacinto as I am
Informed and believe in April of –36
Moreland"

"Is anything else needed?" asked Moreland, as Doctor
Irion looked up over his reading spectacles.

"Is your client with you, Isaac? I would like to meet
her," came the response.

"She is, Your Honor. I will get her." After West entered
the Secretary's office and had been properly introduced, Dr.
Irion spoke. "Miss West, Mr. Moreland has requested a
passport for you. How long have you been in Texas and do
you have your free papers?"

"Sir, I came to Texas from Philadelphia with Captain,
now Colonel, James Morgan in late 1834. I entered into a one-
year contract with him as an indentured servant. That contract
was extended for an additional year, which concluded the end
of December past. I was working for Colonel Morgan when I
was captured at New Washington. The hotel where I lived
was burned and all my belongings, including my free papers,
were lost. I escaped captivity when the Mexicans were
defeated, and I have worked for Captain and Mrs. Moreland
and in the late Vice President de Zavala's household since that
time. With Mr. de Zavala's passing, rest his soul, I now wish
to accompany his widow and her children to the East and will

need a passport to do so."

"Is Colonel Morgan aware of your desire to return east and, if so, does he approve?"

"He is and he does, your Honor", Moreland interjected, "this is a letter of approval from him."

"Very well, Isaac. Miss West, I hereby grant your request." The relief on West's face was noticeable as she bowed slightly in recognition of the State Secretary's action. Dr. Irion then continued. "My clerk will help you and Mr. Moreland with the further paperwork that is required. Let us consider the official date of your request as 15th February 1837. My clerk will notify Mr. Moreland when it is ready."

At the close of their meeting Doctor Irion sat alone in his office. As he tamped fresh tobacco into his pipe bowl and lit up, *he was certain he had just met a living legend - a striking woman with a will of steel - proper papers or not. Whatever her background Emily West was in some way responsible for his and others' ability to exercise power now in the new Republic of Texas.*

"Colonel Morgan, I am ever in your debt for arranging passage for me to travel to New York City with Señora de Zavala and the children. It seems that your kindnesses never end." Emily West stood on the dock at Morgan's Point, addressing her long-time employer and friend.

"How shall I repay you for all you have done for me? I have been in your presence, and under your watchful care for most of the past 12 years. Leaving is so difficult, but the de Zavala family needs my help." Emily West continued, "They require, I believe, a respite from their loss in Texas, and Señora de Zavala wishes to expose the children to New York City and perhaps even take them back to Paris. Señora de Zavala has engaged me to go with them and serve as the children's chaperone. I am excited for the opportunity to go to France - to finally see the land whose language I love. Later who knows! I have missed Philadelphia much more than I thought I would, so I may settle there, and if not there, then New York. But as for Texas, I shall leave her future to you, General Houston and those who look for adventure in new lands. I've had quite enough!"

"Emily, you have been a bright light in my life since the day you arrived at my home in Philadelphia, and I am the one who will miss your presence. But, you are correct, this is an excellent opportunity, not only for you, but for my friend Lorenzo's widow, Emilia and the children. I only trust that whenever possible you make my home your home in Philadelphia. If not, you risk my anger." James Morgan knew as he spoke that *this was probably the last time he would see the young woman he had mentored and admired these last few turbulent years.*

"I will when possible let you know where we are and what we are doing," West responded, her voice hoarse with emotion. "When you are relieved from active duty, which you surely will be soon, I hope you will come to Philadelphia, at least for awhile. Please let me know when you plan to do so and I will be there to meet you."

~

"Buenos días, capitán Bonner. ¿Es este barco navegando oportunidad de Nueva York?" Emilia de Zavala and Emily West spoke almost in unison and smiled at Captain Bonner as he eased the *Flash* against the dock. "Si es así, ¿tiene plazas disponibles para nosotros?"

"Aye, and a good mornin' t' you ladies, and young ones, as well," Captain Bonner replied. "This ship, she's indeed sailin' to New York City. Your berths, th' finest I can offer await you below. Welcome aboard."

Chapter Eighteen

1837-38

Lorenzo de Zavala's untimely death at an early age had shocked and saddened Texans and enraged more than a few in the new republic. He was a hero to most, and the majority reckoned that his death was directly attributable to stress brought about by de Zavala's former comrades and Mexican countrymen. In short - they blamed General Santa Anna and wanted finally to have some frontier justice done. *The little Mexican sonofabitch, Santa Anna, ought to be hanged in a public square!*

Sam Houston, now president of the Republic of Texas, was concerned that Texans might soon take matters into their own hands. To Houston's earlier surprise his old nemesis, President Jackson, had urged him to spare Santa Anna and offered to deal him directly from US custody back to Mexico. So Houston decided to dispatch Santa Anna to Washington as soon as practical, sending him and Santa Anna's trusted associate, Colonel Almonte, overland well to the north in Louisiana to avoid the strong Texan sentiment prevalent in New Orleans. Colonel Almonte spoke perfect English, as well as his native Spanish, and would act as translator. A three-man, heavily armed military escort made up the rest of the contingent. They departed on 25th November 1836, riding cross-country, pitching their own camps through northern Louisiana, and ferrying the Mississippi River at Vicksburg. There they made a pre-arranged rendezvous with a paddlewheel steamer, taking it up the river to Memphis.

News that Santa Anna was aboard the steamboat somehow reached Memphis before he did, and hostile crowds lined the riverbank. Tennesseans were staunchly proud of Sam Houston's victory at San Jacinto. And David Crockett, already a folk hero, had passed through Memphis barely two years earlier, recruiting men who went with him and then dying at the Alamo. Considering the climate it would have been understandable if vigilantes had seized the Mexican general and his military interpreter and lynched them. None of this happened! The steamer anchored 100 yards offshore just long enough to have passengers ferried to and from the docks, then headed swiftly upriver again. The five-man Santa Anna contingent remained below deck.

As the boat made its way north 120 miles or so from Memphis, the landscape along the river changed drastically. The effects of a giant earthquake 25 years earlier were still visible. Santa Anna, now standing on deck and chewing comfortably on a lump of chicle, saw an incredible sight. Trees projected at odd angles from the banks and out of the shallows. Sand blows had heaved the earth upward along the banks. The temblor had caused the ground for miles just east of the Tiptonville hamlet in northwest Tennessee to sink precipitously. At the same time, a two-mile section of the east bank had dropped several feet, and the Mississippi River had run backward for almost two days until it had filled the depression. Just as suddenly, the bank was thrust upward again, and the breach closed, leaving a 40 square mile lake, more than fifteen feet deep in some places, where dry land had existed just weeks before. Nothing like this had ever happened in the recorded history of the new United States.

Santa Anna, too, had been in earthquakes in Mexico. He had felt their power, but he had never seen the remains of an event of this magnitude. And he marveled now too *how this primitive land with other less visible, but equally earthshaking influences, might have produced men like Sam Houston and David Crockett. What forces had somehow moved them to come and fight for Tejas? Why was Crockett so willing to die in defense of a minor Catholic mission in Béxar? How did Sam Houston decide to leave his high positions in Tennessee and Washington politics and move, first to live primitively with Indians and then in Tejas with rebellious Tejanos? And now he, Santa Anna, and his aide, Juan Almonte, were captives of these people and headed for Washington to*

*face yet another Tennessean, Andrew Jackson? What a strange land
- this Tennessee!*

Further up on the west side of the river were the
remains of New Madrid, Missouri - the epicenter of the
violent quake. New Madrid had all but vanished in the
unprecedented violence of the initial rift, and there had even
been reports that the event caused church bells to ring as far
away as Boston. At Cairo, Illinois, a few more miles upriver,
the ship angled her bow eastward into the Ohio River, leaving
the chaotic landscape, and steamed toward Louisville,
Kentucky, where Santa Anna and his party disembarked on
Christmas Day. The remainder of their journey to Washington
was overland, stopping briefly in Maryland for the informal
military court of inquiry that had been ordered by Andrew
Jackson. During that process, one of the US Army observers,
Lieutenant Hitchcock, wrote in his diary:

*"The officers of the court and attendants adjourned and called at
Robusto Hotel and paid their respects to the distinguished stranger.
He is a Spaniard, a slight figure, about 5 ft. 10, of very commanding,
dignified appearance, graceful manner and benign countenance. He
smiled at his misfortunes, and for my life I could not believe he ever
gave the order for the massacre at Goliad."*

Washington, DC: Lopez de Santa Anna was ushered
into the Pesident's office where he now stood uncomfortably
facing Andrew Jackson. His interpreter and comrade in arms,
Colonel Juan Almonte, stood silently at attention at his side.
Neither had been formally introduced to the President nor
had Andrew Jackson acknowledged their presence with
anything other than a brief nod and a grunt. There were
furrows in Jackson's brow as he read and signed papers on the
massive oak desk that separated them. When the President
looked up, he addressed Santa Anna, "So Señor Santa Anna,
you have had several months to consider recent events and

your role in them. Do you have anything to say for yourself since you have been a guest in the Republic of Texas? Any regrets about what sizeable troubles you've caused both my friends in the Republic and the United States?"

"Excellency, President Jackson" - Santa Anna paused to make sure Almonte was ready to translate – "as I made clear to General Sam Houston and President Burnet several months ago, it has been a most regrettable circumstance, this war between Texas and Mexico. Many, no too many, have died on both sides. We are the same people - not Europeans or Chinese or Japanese - we are all North Americans. We should be standing together. I am most sorry that I have taken part in this misadventure. God, I fear, may judge me harshly. I hope you may do otherwise." Jackson listened as he observed Santa Anna's demeanor. *The General, both in speech and posture, appeared contrite. His words as translated by Colonel Almonte had been well thought out and probably extensively rehearsed over his months in captivity. But Andrew Jackson's suspicions were not allayed.*

The dissertation by Santa Anna concluded, the President without further comment, simply read the order he had been reviewing on his desk - an agreement with the Mexican government and endorsed by Jackson for Santa Anna to return to private citizenship in Mexico and to be permitted to join his family still living at his hacienda, *Manga de Clavo*. Weeks later a grateful, subdued General Santa Anna, accompanied by his trusted friend Colonel Almonte, boarded the *USS Pioneer* and sailed from Baltimore harbor for the port of Vera Cruz.

~

Emily West spent the next few months of 1837 helping Emilia de Zavala resettle in New York after their ocean voyage and spending three weeks together touring old haunts of Emilia de Zavala's in Paris and Provence. Both women ached for their departed friend and lover - Lorenzo de Zavala, but neither had spoken a single word of him. Now with the de Zavala family back in New York, West had more time to herself. She had even been able to find her own, small apartment - *true freedom at last*. Weeks earlier Emily West had also tried to contact Lopez de Santa Anna. For some reason she still *felt an attraction to him* and thought *that they might have unfinished business*. But it was not to be. Local officials, suspicious of her inquiries, informed her only that the general was, "no longer welcome in nor residing anywhere in the United States. President Jackson has ordered his repatriation to Mexico."

It was October when Emilia de Zavala invited Emily West the second time for afternoon tea. Their late afternoon discussion, in her apartment overlooking the spacious public area that twenty years later would be known as Central Park, turned to the future. Emilia de Zavala gave West the news. "My dear you have been very kind to us. I, Augustine...we all know what you have sacrificed to help not only my late husband's cause but us, his family, too."

De Zavala continued, "I have plans in some weeks to return to Texas. We miss our life at Zavala's Point. My husband lies there in the ground, alone. We need to go back...not for him, so much as for us. Will you not join us? I know Colonel Morgan would welcome you back, and I can make it easier for you to travel there."

Emily West's response came quickly, almost without thinking. "Madame de Zavala I too miss Señor de Zavala." Taking a sip of tea, she continued. "From the first moment I saw him at the Morgan Mansion I knew that he was destined for great good. When I think of the next hundred years, maybe more, Texas will surely keep his name and yours, the de Zavalas, and your deeds in their hearts. Your husband will be that single star in their flag. But they need not remember me, nor I them. I have no purpose in Texas any more, nor do I ever yearn for its open ranges blanketed with buffalo clover. My place is here in New York."

And so Emilia de Zavala and Emily West parted - in some ways still adversaries, but ones with unspoken bonds too painful to talk about any further.

~

Barely two months into the year, 1838, war clouds again appeared over Mexico - this time precipitated by the old enemy France and its simmering indignity over an old affront to one of its own, a pastry chef with a shop in Mexico City. Because of minor damages to the bakery by federal police ten years earlier, France, through its ambassador, now suddenly demanded an immediate six hundred thousand pesos as reparation and an apology from the government to the store owner, a French citizen. Notably in 1838 the average wage in Mexico City was a bit less than two pesos a day. A further irritant to the French was some two million francs in duties payable to Paris on which Mexico had long ago allegedly defaulted. Needless to say, Mexico refused any form of repayment, and the Pastry War was on.

The French sent a fleet of warships to blockade the Mexican east coast from the Yucatan to the Rio Grande. Furious, President Bustamante finally summoned Santa Anna from his sojourn at Manga de Clavo and somewhat reluctantly gave him command of the army with orders to break the blockade. Leading a charge against French infantry and lancers at Vera Cruz, Lopez de Santa Anna was hit in the leg by grapeshot...a grave wound that required immediate amputation. The conflict was later settled with US and British peaceful intervention while the general recuperated.

Months later General Santa Anna, now outfitted with a new cork and wood prosthesis and accompanied by a presidential dragoon honor guard, stood solemnly at graveside in his full dress uniform. A lone bugler sounded the mournful notes as a second squad of dragoons readied their muskets and fired three volleys over the grave as they had been ordered. General Lopez de Santa Anna saluted crisply as his severed leg was buried with full military honors. The general had used the incident and his bravery under fire to reenter the Mexican political and military scene. It would not be the last time he did so.

~

April 1838: Spring had come to middle Tennessee. The grounds around the Hermitage in Nashville were pink and red with blooming azaleas. Former President Andrew Jackson sat in the loggia, rocking in his favorite chair and reading two somewhat related and disturbing reports - one recent, one from years earlier. *Less than a year before he had essentially pardoned Mexican General Lopez de Santa Anna and packed him off to his home country aboard a US warship. That should have been the end of it. Now if what he was reading in this latest report was accurate, Santa Anna was back into both leading the military and dabbling in politics in Mexico - but was there a real distinction in that country,* Jackson wondered?

Moreover the second document on his desk was the old report from 1815 pertaining to Colonel Joseph Savary resigning his commission. As Jackson somewhat painfully recalled from years ago, *the colonel never forgave him for ordering Savary, then only a young second major and the first black officer in the US military, to have his battalion of Dominican blacks lay down their arms and "assume duties more suited to their race" in and around New Orleans.* Savary had been awarded a personal commendation from then-General Andrew Jackson for helping to rout the British invasion force in January 1815. *In fact I even publicly embraced that French Negro - in the French Quarter!* Jackson recalled. But the New Orleans mayor and nervous whites had eventually prevailed upon General Jackson to expel all armed blacks from the city and surrounding parishes. Savary, *his French Creole sensitivities wounded,* had publicly burned his commendation and gone into hiding with his forces in Barataria - Jean and Pierre Lafitte's old haunt.

Now as Jackson thought about it, *French Dominicans - maybe still led by Savary? - were offering their services to "free Mexican's and Texians in their struggle to keep Texas independent from both Mexico and the United States."* He knew that *this was not the first time Savary had injected his military presence and leadership skills into this conflict between Texas and Mexico. Restless after months of idle silence in Barataria in the 1820s, the colonel had first moved onto Galveston Island, then led forces, including some of Lafitte's men, in and around Matamoros to defeat Mexican Army units fighting Mexican rebels. Some of these shenanigans had probably contributed to Santa Anna's decision to attack Texas in the first instance, and there were even some reports that Colonel Savary had died in that conflict,* reckoned Jackson. *In any event these guerilla-like "colored units" still existed and could influence the coming tides of battle. They needed to be channeled* more productively in the future, and conflict with Mexico was not finished. He'd put a word in President Van Buren's ear that Colonel Savary's unit might again aid the United States - but first Texas would finally need to be annexed. There was no need for another republic on US borders - not even a friendly one. And with that resolved in his mind, Jackson poured another two fingers of sour mash whiskey into the empty glass beside him.

Chapter Nineteen

1845 - 1848

Late in December 1845 President James K. Polk signed the order. It was official! The Republic of Texas had been annexed to the United States as the 28th state. Five months earlier former President Jackson's nephew and namesake, Andrew Jackson Donelson, the US charge de affaires in the Republic of Texas, had presented the American congressional resolution to Texas President, Anson Jones, who had accepted it, subject to his own legislature's approval. With Texas statehood a reality, the United States inherited the long simmering border dispute with Mexico - diplomatic relations were severed, and the seeds of the next war with Mexico were planted.

In San Antonio de Béxar the wounds of the first war with Mexico were just beginning to heal. Native Texans, Tejanos, and Béxarenos, all were eager but apprehensive to become part of the growing United States. Mexican influence and considerable sentiment for keeping close ties with Mexico was everywhere. Not just in San Antonio or Texas itself, but as far away as California, the Arizona Territory and Oregon there were relatives and friends who now wondered what would happen between Mexico and the United States.

Members of the Ruiz household were no exception. Antonio Ruiz, the Alcado of San Antonio during the Battle of the Alamo, watched his aging father go off to the Texas capital as the first senator from Béxar County. His father had been one of 51 men who had secretly signed the original Texas Declaration of Independence and one of only two Tejanos to do so. *Ruiz, the son, prayed silently that the family was on the winning side...that their Catholic God would protect them.* And one of his own young house servants, Benjamin Booker, a freeman originally from Georgia, left to join a horse cavalry unit of the newly formed Texas Militia. He'd tried to sign on with the well-known remnants of Colonel Savary's old Creole battalion, but they were still deep in the bayous of Louisiana, *no telling when they'd be coming out, and Booker wanted to see action - now!*

He was a talented young man - a music lover with a good ear for tunes and fine hands with long fingers for banjo picking and guitar strumming. Antonio Ruiz had given Booker the yellowing paper with the scratched and scribbled writing, *"Emily, Maid of Morgan's Point,"* several months after finding it at the Alamo. Booker had picked at his strings in the evenings at every opportunity until he finally had set it to music. He renamed it, *"My Yellow Rose of Texas"*.

~

In Mexico City President Valentin Gomez Farias, the fourth Mexican president in less than a year, was desperately trying to rally a country that was fragmented, poor and tired of having its sons killed off fighting Anglos. To little avail General Lopez de Santa Anna was once again coaxed out of retirement to lead part of the Mexican Army. The aging general spent most of the next year reneging on agreements he had made in secret earlier with the United States and trying to declare himself president of Mexico - all considerable distractions to Mexican conduct of the war.

At the same time in the US, President Polk authorized the call-up of up to 50,000 men to prepare for and prosecute the war effort. Polk in his mind *would settle for no less than the capture of Mexico City itself and the total capitulation, perhaps even US annexation of Mexico.* The President was determined to rid the western territories - California, Oregon, Arizona, Nevada and others - of Mexican influence. A two pronged military attack strategy was devised and implemented over the next several months - one striking overland through Monterrey to the Mexican capital - the other a seaborne invasion of the California coast from the Pacific. The land assault on the heartland of Mexico would be augmented by a second amphibious force in a flank attack from the Gulf of Mexico.

The Mexican - American War marked a monumental turning point - for the US, for Mexico and for individuals on both sides. Benjamin Booker survived the war as a stable attendant in one of General Winfield Scott's cavalry units. He never fired a shot, but he and 12,000 others became part of the first massive amphibious assault the United States ever launched. Benjamin Booker went ashore somewhere near Vera Cruz in the company of junior officers who would a later earn their place in history in another war - Robert E. Lee, Ulysses S. Grant, and Thomas *later "Stonewall"* Jackson. He and many of his fellow black…and some white…troopers sat in the evenings at fireside, singing of their *"Yellow Rose,"* while Commodore Matthew Perry's naval guns offshore reduced the ramparts around Vera Cruz to rubble.

In New York, thanks to the spread of the telegraph and its relatively instant means of communicating war news, the American victory at Vera Cruz and the subsequent march on Mexico City galvanized New Yorkers to celebrate with a ticker tape parade watched by almost half a million people. Among them, standing on the sidewalk on Madison Avenue that May morning in 1847, was Emily West. She felt that she *had somehow had a part in Texas history and had survived to now witness this massive parade.* But she yearned for *the quieter days along the San Jacinto River…before it all started. She missed seeing the unique characters in the hotel dining room - people like Bowie and Crockett. West wondered too where Turner Metoyer had gone. She even mourned a bit for young Henry B Crockett and reflected on his hopelessly misplaced affections for her.* But the single tear on her cheek was for Lorenzo de Zavala.

~

And it was late September 1847, near the end of the Mexican American War and the approach of the Treaty of Guadalupe Hidalgo, that the little general, Lopez de Santa Anna fought his last battle for Mexico. He tried to intercept a US relief column from Vera Cruz, but by 9th October was still bogged down near the city when he was relieved of his command by yet another Mexican President. Once again Santa Anna was sent away - this time to Jamaica, then on to Colombia. He would never again achieve power or status in Mexico...but he was not done with contributing to history of another, more peaceful kind - in the United States.

Chapter Twenty

1859 – 1865

"I feel that you are all free men. I am a free man, and we can all do as we please. I come here as a friend, and whenever I can serve you, I will do so - therefore let us stand together! Although we differ in color - we should not disagree in sentiment."

(General Nathan Bedford Forrest, CSA, addressing newly arrived African-American troops near Memphis, late stages of the Civil War)

Austin, Texas 1859: the new governor paced the capitol grounds after his inauguration, shaking hands with many who had helped elect him to office. Sam Houston had tried once before, in 1857, to win the governorship and failed. But now the former general and Tennessee Governor had become the first person in United States history to serve as governor of two states - Tennessee and Texas, and as head of a foreign government - the Republic of Texas. *Along the road to this election,* Houston thought, *there had been more than a few bumps - nay, ruts. Even so his life had been largely satisfying so far. He had escaped marriage in Tennessee, impeachment in Congress and death on the battlefield. Now for seventeen years he'd been happily married to an Alabama girl, Margaret Lea. Their house at Cedar Point on Trinity Bay would always feel more like home than the East Tennessee hills he'd left years ago.*

~

Two years into his term, Sam Houston sat at his desk and pondered silently, as he waited for a messenger from Washington to arrive. *He had been at war somewhere, fighting for some cause, all his life,* he thought, *and now as Texas governor, he faced possibly his most serious conflict.* The United States was splitting apart. Fueled by the issue of whether an individual state had the right to rule itself without federal oversight, many Southern states were seceding from the Union. Whether slave ownership should be at all legal, nationally or state by state, became the focal point. Most northern states and the new president, Abraham Lincoln, representing the federal view, thought *secession was treasonous and moreover judged that slave ownership should be abolished - forcibly if necessary.* Most southern states, including Texas, *demanded to keep an individual state's ability to govern itself unequivocally - and to permit slavery.* Sam Houston was a slave owner, but unlike most Texans, he was dead set against secession as a solution. Houston had addressed one session of the Texas Congress with the opening remark - *"a house divided against itself cannot stand."* Abraham Lincoln would later make this pronouncement his.

On this historic February morning Governor Houston waited in his oak paneled office, his cup in hand. He had broken the Laudanum habit years earlier but still liked a sip of Tennessee sour mash in his coffee - for the pain. Just before nine o'clock, Colonel Fredrick Landers, US Army, was quietly ushered into his office through the side door. After brief formalities and a coffee poured for the visitor, the colonel presented the offer he had come to Sam Houston with. "Governor Houston, speaking for President Lincoln, myself and the US Government, we appreciate the courtesy of this most private and urgent meeting. The president recognizes the courage it took to refuse to sign the Texas Act of Secession, as you have done." Houston sipped at his coffee then gestured with his hands to indicate his understanding. His face was lined and grave, but he did not verbally respond to Lincoln's emissary.

Colonel Landers sipped his coffee and continued, "Unfortunately war between the United States and the so-called 'confederacy' is at hand. Though Texas has voted to secede, it has not formally joined this rebellion, and because of your individual act of defiance to this unlawful vote, the United States would be pleased to assist the governor in returning Texas to full statehood. The President has authorized me to inform you he is prepared to immediately dispatch up to 50,000 federal troops to Texas in support of your decision. Partly to this end a call up of over 75,000 men has already begun." Governor Houston was shocked - *flattered* - and chagrined by the United States proposal, as well as by the confidence regarding the secret buildup of forces.

"I personally am most appreciative of President Lincoln's concern for the preservation of the union and the welfare of Texas. And yours and the President's trust in disclosing such security measures is flattering," Houston said. "I assure you that the confidence you have shown will be maintained until my death. Now - though I believe in one nation under God, I can see no benefit for my beloved Texas being the catalyst for yet another murderous war. There must, by heaven, be another means to maintain our unity!" With those remarks, Sam Houston stood, thanked Colonel Landers for his delicate mission and showed the Lincoln courier out of his office. Houston had not only sealed his own political fate, he had effectively put Texas in the Confederacy. Within days, Sam Houston was a private citizen, sitting at home at Cedar Point. Edwin Clark, his former lieutenant governor was the Governor of Texas, and Texas was no longer a US state.

~

It was 16th April 1861 when two Confederate artillery battalions - 50 guns - eight batteries with six eighteen pounders each, firing salvos left to right - with two guns in reserve - began to relentlessly shell the walls of Fort Sumter, South Carolina. The bloody and uncivilized Civil War had begun!

~

Memphis, May 1864: General Nathan Bedford Forrest, Confederate States of America, sat astride his horse awaiting the arrival of elements of Terrel's 37th Texas Cavalry as reinforcements. Forrest was a seasoned cavalry veteran, but he needed help if the South was to have any hope of surviving this massive onslaught from federal troops. Much of the South was in ruins after three years of conflict between the states.

Over half a million men on both sides had already died in the field - at Gettysburg, Antietam, Shiloh, Vicksburg and elsewhere. Military officers who were West Point classmates and had fought alongside each other in the Mexican-American War found themselves plotting opposing combat strategies. Naval warfare had forever changed when two ironclad, steam powered warships met in hostile action for the first time on open seas. The low profile, uniquely turreted Union *Monitor* and the much larger, heavier Confederate *Merrimac* dueled to a standoff near the mouth of the James River, and the federal blockade remained intact - starving out Virginia and other states. In other naval action on the Mississippi River near Cairo, Illinois, the Southerners dragged massive anchor chains across the river to block the progress of Union gunboats.

And as he waited, Forrest felt deeply *that no Southerner, least not he, would've ever reckoned that free blacks in the north would be so eager to punish their southern neighbors. Now from what he was hearing over 85,000 blacks were in the Union ranks, fighting alongside whites - and even a few Indians? But even more surprising - encouraging he had to admit - the advance scouts from Terrel's cavalry had told him to expect 'more than two hundred' free black horsemen in their unit when it arrived. He needed to be ready to somehow welcome them. What could he say? He would be honest! He owed them that much.*

Shortly after noon, General Forrest heard their singing as the 37th rode in - over 500 strong. *The tune was catchy but unfamiliar to him - a lively, uplifting melody about a lost lover - a REAL cavalryman's song,* Forrest thought. But to him it sounded almost as if they were singing two different verses to the same melody - the blacks had their version - the whites had theirs - something about "a yellow rose in Texas - no other darky - *soldier* - knows her - she's the sweetest rose of color - *little rosebud..."*

At the same time General Forrest was moved to ponder *the contrast between the uplifting melody and the somewhat melancholy spirit of the lyrics. Who could have written these words and music? What kind of woman could have inspired these sentiments?* The General had no way of knowing that *it was a song brought to the 37th Texas Cavalry by a young black man from San Antonio de Béxar, or that the woman who had been its inspiration sat alone this day looking out of her apartment window in New York - still missing life at Morgan's Point.*

~

Benjamin Booker, now twenty-nine years of age, had finally been able realize his dream - to enlist in the Army as a horse soldier and not just a stable boy. He hadn't joined the cavalry to fight AGAINST the United States, or FOR Texas or the Confederacy. Benjamin Booker had just wanted to join the fight. And as for Emily West, at home in her apartment in New York – if she'd ever heard the *"Yellow Rose of Texas,"* she had no idea it was about her.

Epilogue

Fact versus Fiction *and speculation*

Phineas Miller and **Eli Whitney**, who invented the cotton gin, were graduates of Yale College in New Haven, CT. and were partners in the cotton gin manufacturing business. Miller however was not the father of Emily Miller - later known as Emily Morgan then Emily West, as presented in the book, but he did marry the widow of General Nathaniel Greene.

Emily D. West (Emily Morgan) was born in New Haven, Connecticut around 1811. She was of mixed race. Her beauty, intelligence and reputed dalliance with Santa Anna while in captivity during the Battle of San Jacinto in April 1836 has been partially documented. She worked in the New Washington Hotel as a housekeeper and as the port logistician for James Morgan until she was captured by Mexican forces when they sacked New Washington.

It is almost certain that sometime in late 1835 or early 1836 she was the inspiration for the lyrics to "Emily, Maid of Morgan's Point" - later rendered as "The Yellow Rose of Texas". As far as it is known, she never heard the song and never learned it was written about her. In March 1837, West was granted new papers and traveled from Texas to New York City. Little is known about the rest of her life, including where she lived, her marital status, and when or where she died. A hotel in San Antonio is named The Emily Morgan.

Sally Hemings was born in 1773 and lived at Monticello. In 1787, she was chosen to accompany Mary "Polly" Jefferson to Paris to join her father, Thomas Jefferson, where he was serving as minister to France. In 1788, Jefferson took Sally as his concubine, and they had a 38-year relationship that produced six children. Sally died in 1835. Emily West however was never part of the Jefferson household.

Lorenzo de Zavala, born in 1788 in Yucatán, New Spain, was an extraordinary scholar, politician, physician, and entrepreneur. His political service included election to several offices in the Mexican government, ambassador to France for Mexico, and interim vice president of the newly independent Republic of Texas in 1836. He married Teresa Correa in 1807 and they had two children. After her death in 1831, he married Emilia West *[the authors firmly believe there were two Emily/Emilia Wests]* with whom he had three children. He died from pneumonia in November 1836 and was buried in the family cemetery at Zavala's Point, Texas. He drew the sketch for one of the first official flags of the Republic of Texas. There is no evidence he ever met or had a relationship with Emily West (Morgan), the legendary heroine of the Battle of San Jacinto.

Antonio de Padua Mario Severino Lopez de Santa Anna y Perez de LeBron was born in Xalapa, Vera Cruz, New Spain, to a respected Spanish colonial family on 21st February 1794. He became a political leader, general, and president who greatly influenced early Mexican and Spanish politics and government. Santa Anna fought first against Mexican independence from Spain, then in support of it. He held the rank of general and/or the office of president, sometimes concurrently, several times over a turbulent 40-year career. He was president of Mexico on eleven non-consecutive occasions over a period of 22 years. He was infamous for his involvement in the massacres at the Alamo and Goliad. He was humiliated at the Battle of San Jacinto, which led to the independence of Texas. After the US Civil War Santa Anna was again living in New York when he convinced his landlord, Thomas Adams, to accept one ton of Mexican chicle as rent payment. Adams wanted to use the chicle, a latex product, to replace steel wagon wheel rims. The experiment failed, but Adams and friends used the chicle to produce the first commercial chewing gum in the United States - Chiclets. Santa Anna, nearly blind from cataracts, died in Mexico City on 21st June 1876.

James Morgan after his duties on Galveston Island, returned to his Morgan's Point plantation and built a new home, The Orange Grove. During the 1850s Morgan was active in promoting the improvement of what later became the Houston Ship Channel. He owned extensive herds of cattle and experimented with the cultivation of oranges, cotton, and sugarcane. Morgan was completely blind during his last years. He died at his home on 1st March 1866, and is buried in the family cemetery.

Renato Beluche was a merchant sea captain and successful privateer. He was Simón Bolívar's favorite admiral and a partner in the affairs of the Lafitte brothers. He joined with Jean Lafitte to aid General Andrew Jackson during the British invasion of the Gulf Coast during the War of 1812. He died peacefully in Puerto Cabello, Venezuela in 1860. The events in the book describing Beluche's exploits in relation to the *Flash* and the Morgan party however are fictional.

John Jacob Houseman was in the wrecking business in Key West. In 1831, he developed a more favorable port of entry, admiralty court and customs house on Indian Key and set up a mini-empire under his own control. Indian Key under Houseman became the first county seat of Dade County. In 1840, his island was attacked by a large party of Indians during the Seminole War. Housman escaped, but his Indian Key empire was in ashes. **Doctor Henry Perrine**, who had moved to the island to raise agave for hemp, hid his family in a turtle kraal under Houseman's quarters during the Seminole attack. They survived but Perrine was killed while trying to negotiate with the Indians. Housman died in rough seas off the coast of Key West in 1841 while trying to salvage two ships.

Alexis de Tocqueville, a French political liberal and ardent student of American democracy, traveled the eastern United States with his friend **Gustave de Beaumont** in the 1830s. Although they did study the US prison system, the two men were more broadly interested in the overall political system, slavery and military prowess. De Tocqueville penned a well-known two-volume work, "Democracy in America," between 1836 and 1840 and is often quoted by political historians. He and de Beaumont visited Cincinnati, but there is no evidence they influenced the city to dispatch the "Twin Sisters" artillery pieces to San Jacinto. Even so the two cannons, gifts from the people of Cincinnati, indeed helped turn the tide of battle for Sam Houston's forces. There is no evidence that de Tocqueville or de Beaumont ever met Morgan, West or de Zavala.

Benjamin Strobel, was born in 1803 in Charleston, South Carolina, and graduated from the Medical College of South Carolina in 1826. He was an amateur naturalist and acquainted with John Audubon. He lived in the Florida Keys, including Indian Key, during the late 1820s and early 1830s. He wrote for the Key West Gazette and was one of the best-informed men in the Keys. He returned to Charleston in 1833 and entered medical practice. Strobel participated in the Second Seminole War with the South Carolina Volunteers for three months in 1836 as a regimental surgeon. His last known trip to Florida, to St. Augustine during its yellow fever epidemic, was in 1839. He died at his brother-in-law's house in Charleston in 1849.

Sam Houston, a Tennessee native and hero of the Texas Revolution, was twice elected President of the Republic of Texas; and once to the Texas House of Representatives, the U. S. Senate, and as the governor of Tennessee and Texas. Houston was evicted from the Texas governor's seat in March 1861 for refusing to take an oath of loyalty to the Confederacy. He developed pneumonia and died on 26th July 1863. He is buried in Huntsville, Texas. The city of Houston, Texas was named in his honor, along with numerous other public buildings, schools and hotels. Houston indeed had a serious confrontation with Colonel James Morgan over Morgan's conduct of the defense of Galveston Island in 1836.

Francisco Antonio Ruiz was Alcado (mayor and city magistrate) of San Antonio de Béxar during the Alamo battle. He was placed under house arrest by Santa Anna prior to the battle because of his Tejano background and sentiments. Ruiz was later forced to identify bodies of many of those killed at the Alamo. His father, Jose Franciso Ruiz, traveled to Washington-on-the-Brazos in February 1836 and was one of only two Tejanos to sign the Texas Declaration of Independence. As a senator he represented the Béxar district in the First Congress of the Texas Republic. He is buried in

San Antonio. The younger Ruiz did not however find or take the original handwritten lyrics to "Emily, Maid of Morgan's Point" from a body after the Alamo battle.

Emilia West de Zavala returned to New York City in March 1837. She remarried a German immigrant and returned to Texas and Zavala's Point in 1839. She remained there until 1870, when she moved to Galveston, where her eldest son, Augustine, lived. She sold the land at Zavala's Point to her second son, Richard. Emilia died 15th June 1882 in Houston and was buried in the family cemetery at Zavala's Point, Texas.

Andrew Jackson, born in South Carolina of Scotch-Irish parents, was the hero of the Battle of New Orleans in the War of 1812, a member of Congress from Tennessee, a justice on the Tennessee Supreme Court and Governor of the Florida Territory before becoming US President. He was a staunch advocate of the Union and pressed relentlessly for US expansion. On 30th January 1835 Jackson became the first US President to survive an assassination attempt when Richard Lawrence's weapons both misfired. He died at the Hermitage in Nashville 8th June 1845 and is buried on the grounds.

Jim Bowie and **David Crockett,** well known frontiersmen from Louisiana and Tennessee, died at the Alamo. Crockett was in Washington in Congress with Sam Houston when Andrew Jackson was President. Bowie and Jean Lafitte were on Galveston Island together in the early 1800s. Crockett killed bears - over 600 one winter in West Tennessee and fed most of the local population. His favorite long rifle was a gift to him from a wealthy Philadelphia admirer, but probably not James Morgan. Jim Bowie and his brothers invented several versions of the legendary Bowie knife and were known to use them in local Louisiana fights.

Captain Isaac Moreland came to Texas in 1834 and commanded the artillery at the Battle of San Jacinto. He was the law partner of David Burnet and assisted Emily D. West in obtaining a new passport that allowed her to return to New York City after the Battle of San Jacinto. He died in 1842.

Colonel Juan Almonte, a Mexican official, soldier and diplomat, was born in 1803 in the state of Michoacán. He was educated in New Orleans, where he learned English. In January 1836, Almonte was appointed aide-de-camp to Antonio López de Santa Anna and accompanied him to Texas. At the Battle of San Jacinto, Almonte led the last organized resistance of the Mexican army. He was taken prisoner and stayed with Santa Anna during his imprisonment, acting as interpreter and negotiator - accompanying Santa Anna to Washington, D.C. to meet with President Andrew Jackson. They left the U.S. in late January 1837 and returned to Mexico aboard the *USS Pioneer*. Almonte continued his diplomatic and military career and eventually rose to the rank of major general. He ultimately fled to Europe and spent his last days in exile, dying 21st March 1869.

Colonel Mirabeau Lamar, born in 1798 in Georgia, became a Texas politician, diplomat and soldier during the Texas Republic era. He was accepted to Princeton, but chose not to attend. He joined Sam Houston's army in the spring 1836 and distinguished himself at the Battle of San Jacinto, where he commanded the cavalry. His actions at the battle led to an appointment as the Secretary of War in the interim Texas government. He was the third president of the Republic of Texas after David Burnet had served in an interim role and Sam Houston served the first full term. He initially opposed Texas annexation to the United States. Lamar returned to military service after Houston was elected to his second term as president in 1841. He distinguished himself at the Battle of Monterrey during the Mexican-American War. He represented Eagle Pass in the Texas State Legislature for several years after Texas was annexed to the United States. In 1857, President James Buchanan appointed Lamar to be the Minister to Nicaragua. After 20 months in Managua, he returned to Texas because of poor health. He died at his Richmond plantation in December 1859.

Doctor Robert A. Irion served as a senator in the first congress of the Republic of Texas in 1836-37 and served as Secretary of State for the Republic of Texas in 1837-38. He was Sam Houston's personal physician. Dr. Irion's endorsement of Isaac Moreland's handwritten request for a passport for Emily D. West to travel to New York in 1837 is a matter of record from the Texas State Library and Archives Commission.

Joseph Savary was a native of Saint-Dominque (Haiti) and, like Andrew Jackson, was a hero of the Battle of New Orleans. Savary's Second Battalion, Free Men of Color of the Louisiana Militia, some 256 men, was incorporated into the United States Army to fight against the British on 19th December 1814. Savary was promoted to the rank of second major and became the first black officer in the history of the U.S. Army. The Second Battalion's first battle occurred four days later when it fought back the British who were attempting to enter the city. Savary's battalion defied orders and rushed to the front to participate in the rout of British forces. That rout began when one of Savary's men killed British Commanding General Pakenham on the field of battle. At the end of the conflict General Andrew Jackson publicly praised the Second Battalion and its commander. When the war ended, however, Jackson yielded to the pressure of New Orleans's white residents and ordered all black troops out of the city. Savary and his men saw the removal orders as a racial affront. He and many of them returned to Spanish Texas where they were welcomed by Pierre Lafitte. Savary and his men joined Mexican rebels fighting for their nation's independence. His return to the US and eventual demise is unclear, but Savary was listed as living in New Orleans in 1822.

John Smith, Captain Robert Bonner, Nipper and Sarah Grigsby, Pierre Crump, Constable Nathan Wilson, Benjamin Booker, Turner Metoyer, (Emily West's accomplice at the Battle of San Jacinto), and Henry Baynes Crockett are fictional characters. Henry Crockett, in the book, is the author of "Emily, Maid of Morgan's Point." Though it is believed that a young slave or freeman, probably from Tennessee, penned the words and left the initials HBC on the work, the true author has never been identified.

Chapter Twenty: The narrative suggesting that African-Americans joined the 37th Cavalry and fought actively for the South has never been conclusively documented in reliable military records. However the words attributed to **Confederate General Nathan Bedford Forrest** have been substantially documented as remarks he made to African-Americans, either conscripts or volunteers, about to enter the fight against Union troops on the outskirts of Memphis, late in the Civil War.

"Yellow Rose of Texas": There are at least three different versions of lyrics and verses to *"The Yellow Rose of Texas."* The original lyrics are thought to be as described in Chapter Twelve and carried the title, *"Emily, Maid of Morgan's Point."* The version in this book represents a portion of the unpublished, handwritten document - a part of the University of Texas Archives from around 1836.

Béxar: historically the strategically important region in central Texas surrounding San Antonio, now Béxar County.

Tejas, Texian and **Tejano:** "Tejas" is a Spanish derivation of the original Caddo tribe word for "friend" or "ally." The Spanish borrowed the term from the indigenous peoples to describe what is now Texas when they first explored and settled the region. The term "Texian" refers to any resident of Mexican Texas or later the Republic of Texas. "Tejano" generally refers to any Spanish speaking Texan of the period, or in some cases regionally, to Hispanicized German immigrants to Texas in the 1800s.

About the Authors:

Robert Wuench and Howard Carman were both born in Tennessee. Their early years were shaped by life in a small town, Union City, in northwest Tennessee - *David Crockett territory*. They and their families have been close friends for more than a half-century.

The authors both have engineering backgrounds. Carman is a registered professional engineer and a former vice chancellor of The University of Tennessee. He has traveled in Texas often and, with his wife, resides in Memphis. Wuench is a former US Army armored cavalry officer. He worked and traveled internationally for more than 20 years with Caterpillar Inc. and lived ten years in Houston as executive vice president of a Mitsubishi Heavy Industries venture. He and his wife live in Solon, Ohio.

Thorn of Béxar is the authors' first novel. They were inspired to write it because both appreciate the close historical relationship between the *Volunteer State* and the *Lone Star State*, forged in the War for Texas Independence. Both men have always enjoyed a good story and believe this is one worth telling.

Made in the USA
Lexington, KY
05 June 2012